THE
GREAT RETURN

VOLUME TWO
MAKA SHAN SAGA

THE
GREAT RETURN

VOLUME TWO:
MAKA SHAN SAGA

Written by
Anatarra Whitewing

Afterword by
Dr. Angela Browne-Miller

Metaterra® Publications

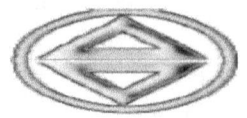

metaterra®
publications

THE GREAT RETURN
Volume Two: Maka Shan Saga

Published in the United States by Metaterra® Publications.
www.Metaterra.com
Library of Congress Cataloging-in-Publication Data.
Whitewing, Anatarra. Browne-Miller, Angela.
The Great Return/Anatarra Whitewing/Angela Browne-Miller – 1st Edition.
1. Fiction. 2. Women. 3. Romance. 4. Mythology. 5. Psychology.
6. Adventure. 7. Spiritual/Theology/Metaphysical/Esoteric. 8. Native
American/Indigenous. 9. Paranormal.
Title:
The Great Return
Volume Two: Maka Shan Saga
Library of Congress Control Number: (see website listed above)
ISBN-13: 978-1-937951-02-3 (Paperback)
ISBN-13: 978-0-9645472-7-8 (Kindle eBook)
Published in the United States of America for US and worldwide
distribution.
Metaterra® Publications, 1 Blackfield Dr 343, Tiburon, CA 94920, USA.
Cover and content illustrations by and copyright ©Angela Browne-Miller.
Book design by and copyright ©Angela Browne-Miller.
Ordering information and bulk ordering information available through
Amazon, Kindle, Barnes and Noble, Google, and Apple iBook distributors.
Also contact Info@Metaterra.com.

PUBLISHER'S NOTE

*Dedicated to those
who are here for
the
Great Return.*

Everyone.

Volume Two: Maka Shan Saga

TABLE OF CONTENTS

part one:

search for the sacred

Volume Two: Maka Shan Saga

1.
free

Everything looked different now.

I had just had a confusing, disturbing, painful, yet most inspiring life-changing journey into a world I had not known was there. Not exactly anyway. While my youth had been checkered with apparent contact experiences – contact with the world beyond the physical plane – I had been unable to place it all into any clarifying context. Furthermore, I had lost my mother less than a year earlier, and now it seemed she was somehow reaching me from the other side. She was showing up from time to time, as Sveeka, some sort of ghost or magical priestess or something.

There were times I questioned all this, telling myself this was only the imagination of a sad teenager, the longing of a confused young mind. But I had to admit to myself that I was most likely, no, probably even actually, seeing the veils between dimensions of reality eroding away, revealing what was actually truth. Or someone's truth.

I was indeed confused, confused but determined to figure all this out. Figuring this out became a compulsion, one which drove the next several chapters of my life, if not my entire life – at least on some level.

I had recently miscarried the baby of a tribal leader, a man named Fire Star. I had barely made it. Thank goodness for that last minute rescue from that isolated commune. I was rushed to the hospital and I lived.

The moment I stepped outside the hospital, I realized I was free. Almost dead, but free. It was the first time I ever really appreciated "freedom," or at least the illusion of it.

But here I was, back in the white world, the day world – land of the paper people and the dead ground. Almost instantly after walking out of the hospital building, reverse culture shock set in. I was frantic – all the magic I had found while living with the tribe seemed gone from my life. And I would spend the next few years banging urgently on the door of the spirit realm, trying to get back in. I would search high and low for a better, cleaner, more protected opening than the one I had found at the Tribe – an opening that would allow me safe passage back to where I had been able to touch my higher origins, my cosmic home.

It would be quite a while before I would realize that I was already there, that I had been standing there, here, already before all this. We all are standing there, here, at the threshold and even already within, the spirit realm – the realm to the higher levels of our consciousnesses.

My search began that very night. I stood there in the street, sick and stranded – damaged. The chemistry of the ancient reality I had touched, after paying the high price of admission, now seemed to pop and disappear in mid air like a thin-skinned bubble. It seemed that the spirits I had come to know so well were receding, rapidly, like winds rushing directly away from me in all directions. I wanted to stop these spirits from abandoning me, but I felt too weak. I wanted to call them back, to reach out and to hold them there, but the city was too loud and the air too thick. Would they ever come back for me? Would I spend the rest of this life alone here? (At that stage of my life, I could not see the answers. I like to think I can, now.)

The Earth herself seemed far away now, even though I knew her soil was just a few inches beneath the pavement. A garbage truck rolled by, reeking of rot, with heavy metallic rock music coming from its windows. I reeled, almost fainting, at the stench of this existence. My head was pounding and my uterus contracting – my baby was dead.

My baby was dead! With this realization, a searing slash ran through my guts. As I doubled over, Mark put his arm around me to steady me. We hugged in our shared angst, disillusionment, and burst dreams of Fire Star Tribe utopia, trying to drown out the sirens, horns, harsh voices, and slamming doors.

"You need to sit down," Mark said, stepping me over to a bench. I resisted. "Sit," he insisted. I did. "Lilith … man, Akashakana, we're going to take you home before we go," he said. I saw Jim nod in agreement.

I could see they cared, they really did. And Mark seemed to have finally understood that Chief Fire Star had forced me to have sex with him, or I never would have. Bringing out a loaded weapon, and making it clear it was loaded while I was trying to say no, was force. No one could see this as otherwise. Mark had come to know this. So had Jim.

I scowled and looked at them, insulted. How could they leave me now? Weren't they my dear friends? Hadn't we been through all this together? But it was hard to be angry at these two young men, practically still just boys, the same age as I was. Innocent "half-breed Mark" as he called himself and tall scraggly-haired waif-like "bean stalk Jim" as he was known: they both looked pale and drawn, very worried about me. And they looked lost. They were obviously as disoriented as I was after leaving the Tribe. We weren't kids, we were in our late teens, which we thought was quite mature, but we had recently encountered and seen far more than many times our years. And now look where we were. Where? Where? In the grand scheme of things, it felt like nowhere. Now we were more confused than ever.

"You're going to go?" I demanded, trying to act well although I was still extremely weak after losing so much blood. "Go where?"

"Hopping freights to the East coast," Jim offered almost apologetically. "I need to get home and see my parents. They've probably got the FBI or the CIA or something like that out looking for me by now." Jim had never mentioned that his father actually was a CIA agent, a de-briefer. And Jim didn't offer this information now, either. It would be quite some time before this came out. It would also be quite some time before it became clear that Jim was several years older than David and I were. Jim was not eighteen, not at all.

16

Somehow he was able to fool us back then. But why? What was he really up to? I would not figure this out for quite some time.

But we were virtually still kids. Sort of.

My head kept pounding. "You guys are crossing the country? Without me? What kind of friends are you?"

"You can't do it. You're sick," Mark tried to comfort me. "We'll come back for you, I promise. The doctor said you have to go home."

"Home?" What on Earth did they mean by home? There was a gnawing in my heart. How could I go back and face what remained of my so-called biological family after this? How could I bring myself to tell my family what had happened? Shame raced through me. No way could I face my father.

"Yeah, you won't make it. It's a real rough trip," Jim chimed in. "But we'll miss you like hell."

"I won't make it? Just watch me."

Mark and Jim stared at me, not knowing what to do with my new level of assertiveness. I went on. "Come on, you guys, don't be ridiculous. Neither of you would have made it through what I just went through, so don't tell me what I can and can't do."

Mark looked sad, hurt, and very concerned. "This is ridiculous. If you bleed anymore you'll die. They said to stay in bed for a month. … Come on, really, you know I love you and want you okay."

"No way I'll do that." I tried to laugh but I ached too much to manage it. I pressed on my abdomen, hoping to still the rugged wave of uterine contractions that had just hit. The pain was surprising – the miscarriage was over. What was this?

"Come on, don't be hurt. We both care about you a lot. It's just that … that…." Jim couldn't explain what was on his mind so David did it for him. "What are we going to do if you start to hemorrhage out in the middle of nowhere, days away from anything? You could die."

I stood up to stand my ground. "If I'm not already dead, I won't be dying soon. If I am dead, then what does it matter?"

"Come on, really. What are we going to do if you die?" Mark pleaded.

"Just throw my body off the train. I won't need it anymore." That was it. As far as I was concerned, the matter was resolved. Anyway, I was mostly dead already. I moved to the curb, stuck out my thumb and started the hitchhike for them. None of us noticed we were being watched. None of us noticed that the person watching us was taking pictures with a very tiny camera. It would be quite a while before what this was about would be known – it would be a very long time, almost lifetimes later.

We had little trouble catching rides. It was the 1970s and young people hitchhiking were still considered safe, whether or not they really were. As usual, drivers were far more likely to stop for females with or without males than males without females. Mark and Jim would stand back and usually sit down while I would get people to stop to give me the ride, and then I'd ask politely if there was room for my friends. If I got a yes, they'd follow me in. My dogged pilgrimage to a seeming nowhere – the next level of my awareness disguised as nothing – had begun.

Eventually we made it to the Los Angeles freight yards and waited until we could secretly climb into an open boxcar. Back then, this wasn't too hard to do. Getting off the train was the problem. The train didn't really stop long enough for us to climb down or even jump off at all safely until Sanderson, Texas, a border town where the "ole' USA" ended and Mexico began. By then we all were sick. Maybe Flower and Tree Dog's hepatitis and trench mouth, so common back up there in that tribal commune, had become ours now, even though we three had been careful about sharing water with members of the Tribe.

We snuck out of the Sanderson train yard and hiked into town to a gas station. I immediately went into the ladies' room and tried to wash my thick longer than elbow-length hair, which was forming its own version of natty dreads. The filth was infinite, and I eventually gave up. For the rest of the trip, I packed my hair into David's old ski hat. With David's ragged leather coat on, its shoulders far wider than mine, I could pass for a boy. This, I had come to realize, was a good idea. A freight yard was no place for a female. It didn't seem to be a place for spirits, either. At least I had found no sign of them there. Not so far.

We waited until it was very dark and then snuck back into the freight yards. We found an open boxcar and climbed in. We crouched in the far and darkest corner, wondering how long it would be before they would begin to move the train. Finally there was a grinding and a metallic wheeze, and the train groaned and moved a few inches. But then it stopped again.

We heard footsteps and a scrambling sound.

"What was that?" I gasped.

"Don't know," Mark whispered through clenched teeth.

"Shhh," Jim warned.

"Could they arrest us?" I wondered.

"Don't know."

"You mean this could really be against the law?" I asked.

"Don't—"

Just then, a gnome-like man, unbelievably balled-up like a package of strange energy, wearing a business suit of all things, a suit over many layers of clothes, carrying a large piece of cardboard, came out of nowhere and hurtled himself into our boxcar. When he landed, he glanced behind him out the train door as if he were running from something. He grabbed his cardboard and his hat, which had fallen off as he leapt in, and scurried to the other corner of the boxcar to hide in the dark. He seemed to disappear there, his shape melting to the form of the dark corner into which he had disappeared.

"Where did he go?" I squinted trying to see what he had done to hide himself. But Mark and Jim were more concerned with who else was coming our way. We said nothing as we saw the flicker of flashlight beams approaching and then heard several heavy feet stomping through the gravel alongside the train. We could hear each other gulp.

"Oh shit," Jim whispered almost silently.

I nudged him with a quiet "shhh," and began to chant, just as quietly, a prayer I had heard my dear friend and teacher, Kiowa, say many times back up on tribal land. *"Hey lo, hey yah. .... Hey hey hey..."*

Next we knew, the flashlight beams hit us. I leapt up, put my hands in the air as if I were being arrested, and went to the doorway of the car. Surprised at my behavior, Mark and Jim followed suit so as not to appear as if they were hiding while I wasn't.

The lights were in our eyes. "Kids. Just kids, white kids," the man with the light said. He sounded disappointed.

"What're you kids doin' here?" a broad Texas drawl demanded.

"Trying to get home, that's all," Mark told him.

"Any of you kids seen a Mexican runnin' by?"

"Nope."

"No."

"Uh uh," the three of us answered with me hiding the female in my voice behind the louder tones of Mark and Jim. I didn't want these guys to know I was a girl. I wasn't sure why.

"Well you're damn lucky that's who we're after tah-night."

"Next time take a bus. You kids shouldn't be around places like this."

"Yes, sir."

"Okay."

"Yep," we said.

They walked off, angrily searching car after car, and finding nothing.

The gnome who had disappeared into the corner was still invisible – missing. It was as if he wasn't there. There was no sign of his moving, mumbling, or even breathing until the train moved and picked up speed. Then he emerged – really far too abruptly for this to have been a natural movement – out of nowhere, as if there had been a doorway in the air for him to come through. Maybe I was just scared and exhausted, or lonely for someone who would help me find what I desperately needed (whatever that was), but it seemed that this man knew some of my dear friend Kiowa's magic.

He laid his cardboard out flat on the filthy floor of the train. He took his hat off and dusted it. He took his jacket off, carefully turned it inside out, and then folded it into a pillow shape. He crouched on his cardboard and murmured rhythmically to himself.

I stared at him. He caught my eye in the moonlight, and seemed to suddenly realize something about me – I assumed it was that I was a girl. He did nothing overt in response, but he nodded at me and began to chant a little louder in what I recognized as an indigenous man's language. He added a bit of melody. I even thought I had heard his tune before, back among the people of the Tribe. How could that be?

I rocked to the rhythm of his song, just a little. I needed this shred of comfort. This sort of ritual was a part of tribal life that I already missed.

And so we traveled. I spent the moonlit night transfixed by that man's ongoing private ceremony. Long before morning light, I realized he was indeed a Native American, but not of the more northern tribes I had come to know through the Fire Star Tribe. He was indeed summoning the spirits. Maybe he had indeed come from Mexico, I didn't know. But the modern borders were clearly irrelevant to him. He lived in old time. And he walked in two worlds, the here and the there.

The night was intolerably long, unending. The ride was nasty. We all took a beating. It was way too much for me in my horrid physical condition. It was so bumpy that my body hit the floor real hard thousands of times, each time after being tossed about a foot into the air, which was every few seconds or so. I felt like I was having a baby, with no break in the labor pains. I wanted to throw myself out the train doorway to end it all – it seemed I was about to hemorrhage again. Looking back, it was as if I was giving birth to myself.

As the sun brought a glorious but mostly ignored dawn to the horizon, we were just passing a missile silo out in the middle of nowhere. I was feeling on the verge of death – my now frequent companion – again, my uterus contracting in increasingly fierce spasms. I was already curled up in fetal position, but now I crunched up even tighter and started screaming in pain with each bounce of the train. Mark and Jim were terrified. I figured this was the end for me. So did they. Mark was starting to cry. Mark was a big strong young man and tears did not come to him very often, or very easily.

The pain was too much to tolerate. My mind was jumbled and I was slipping in and out of a feverish delirium. I was in so much agony that I grew confused about its cause. I kept feeling as if I was being torn open and my heart was being ripped out in preparation for my being thrown down from the train and into a dark pool. It was as if I had already experienced this bloody sacrifice, knew it well, and was ready to do it again. I kept thinking that there really was a pool full of dark water and that I was really wanting to be thrown into it. And then I kept telling myself I was just feverish, that I was on a train running over firm ground, and that no one was ripping my heart out – that I was just grieving my baby. Or dying due to lost blood.

I'm not sure when the gnome appeared by my side, singing and chanting, but I found myself grabbing his hand. I was aware that Mark and Jim didn't want him to touch me, but I was also aware that try as they might to keep him away, they were absolutely powerless to stop him. There was no logical explanation for this. He was a very small man.

He mumbled something I couldn't understand and unfolded me a bit. He put his free hand over my abdomen and looked upward. Then he made several vertical motions with that hand, as if he were removing something from me. The pain reduced by well over half immediately. My moans grew quieter. Then he made some motions resembling an effort to suck something out of my abdomen. He blew it away, out the door of the train.

I was so dumbfounded, I forgot I was in pain. Or maybe the pain went away. What had he done? And where had Mark and Jim gone? The train was still moving. No one could have gotten off of it. But they were nowhere. Next I knew, I was dizzy. The boxcar was spinning. And then things were a rushing sort of still.

Now, the three of us, Mark, Jim and I, were sitting in the doorway of the racing train, watching the world go by, and the gnome man was back in his corner, hunched over. I could remember what had just happened. I could remember being in excruciating pain. I could remember dying and being saved by the gnome, but it was as if none of this had ever happened. I said nothing about all this. It was as if the gnome wanted me to say nothing.

"Where are we?" Jim asked.

"Don't know," Mark replied.

"Could be days and days more of this endless travel, you know," Jim told him.

"Yep."

Mark pulled out some crackers and an orange. He split the orange among the three of us and gave us each a few crackers.

"What about him?" I asked, tilting my head toward the little man hunched in the other corner.

"What do you mean what about him?"

"He's probably hungry, Mark."

"Let him be. He could be armed," Mark insisted.

I made a face at Mark and then looked at the man and shouted loudly over the sound of the train, "*Tiene hambre*?" I said, figuring he spoke Spanish. Are you hungry?

The man jerked his head around and looked at me.

"What are you doing?" Mark was irritated.

"Seeing if he wants some food," I answered. "I'm sure we can spare a little."

The man was still looking at me. He smiled just a bit and shook his head no. Then he pulled a loaf of bread out of a paper sack he had and offered me some. I shook my head no and smiled. Right then, a single ray of the rising sun hit his eyes and I got a good look at them. There was a flicker of the spirit world, the world that I thought had left me when it floated off in the bubble of tribe life, the bubble that had popped. I could tell, I just knew, he knew the magic of the ancient realm.

I had to touch the magic that was lurking in his eyes. I had to get him to open up and share with me the key, directions to the portal to the non-physical realm, the spirit world, to that world I longed to re-enter. I crawled over and tried to begin a conversation with him about this.

All he would say to me was, "*Ya tienes, ya tienes, tu tienes la llave.*"

What could he mean by telling me that I already had it? That I already had the key? He never explained. Instead of getting answers, I discovered that he was craftily elusive, or so I thought at the time. It seemed to me that he kept that magic well-protected and, for safety, quite hidden. So instead we just talked in Spanish about what we were all doing there in that filthy boxcar.

By the time we approached St. Louis, I had been translating as best I could for him as he explained to us that this was the train his people took to get in from Mexico and make their way to Chicago. They were an old, old line of roaming *vagabondos*, vagabonds, he said. He added that this is what *"los elitos,"* the elite, had called them. His people did not understand the ways of modern borders. The old Earth where his people had lived for many many centuries and had built a great civilization, knew no US-Mexico boundaries. His people had no country but planet Earth now, he said. Even though his people had once developed great settlements around their pyramid-like temples, their nomadic life was natural back then. But now, when they crossed the modern boundaries, they knew they risked ending up in white jails and being shipped south for further punishment, as many of them had.

It was worth the risk he told us. His people were dying of malnutrition back home. Their spirits were almost gone. Their spirits were dying in the modern world. He said that now Mexican, Central American and South American officials were, on ancient ritual days, standing around the ancient temples and sacred lands with guns, trying to prevent the medicine men and priests from summoning their ancient gods for help. Now their spirits couldn't save them from the problems of being here in this time in history, on this dying planet.

So the gnome-man needed to make the money here in the US and then take it home to save his people. The money would help them work their magic again. Or at least keep them from becoming an entirely extinct race. He seemed to add that his people needed to survive to help heal the Earth. He said that Earth was crying out for help saving his people. And vice versa.

He said this was war … war to save the *Pachamama*, Mother Earth, from those killing her. War to save the sacred portals on material Earth, openings, lifelines, to the sacred dimensions of higher Earth. He told stories of sacred portal doorways now receding for safekeeping, and sacred portal doorways being destroyed by commercialism, and sacred portal doorways that had already fallen under government and military control. I could feel that these were the doorways I longed to find, I just could tell. But directions to them were not forthcoming. At least it seemed this was the case.

By the time he had said this much, I was not surprised to hear that he believed this time to be the beginning of the predicted Great War, the war we would see come to fruition many years later. I had already learned about the predicted Great War when I lived with the Fire Star Tribe. And I had also learned this long before. Eons earlier. *(What I was still going to learn was how this Great War was truly taking place on many dimensions, and was part of the Great Rebalancing. The Great War would not have to be physically violent, if humanity could come to understand this in time.)*

Unless we could work with *Maka* to change this, life on Earth and maybe even the life of Earth would die.

Was this the end of time he was talking about?

The Great Rebalancing?

I shuddered, awash in a truth I could not yet make sense of.

2.
sky loom

It was sundown when we landed in St. Louis.

The gnome-man needed to get off the train and walk into town there, he told us. He had to catch a bus to Chicago. We said goodbye and gave him one of our sleeping bags, two shirts and twenty five dollars, which is about half of what we collectively had. He bowed to us in gratitude and then, at the doorway of the boxcar, chanted and prayed before climbing down. Obviously he was praying to the spirits for protection. Seeing this, the idea to go with him came into Mark's, Jim's and my mind at exactly the same moment. Which was good of us, but a rather dangerous idea.

We all climbed down. The gnome-man touched my hand and nodded upward. I glanced directly up just in time to see a short straight strip of an extremely bright rainbow span a small cloud looming alone in the sky. Its brilliance struck my retinas with some kind of supernatural force, the same way a rainbow strip back up on tribal land had. A medicine woman had called the rainbow forth during a dawn fertility ceremony she had led for the Tribe. It too had loomed directly overhead, alone in the sky.

29

"*Siete rayes,*" the gnome said in a low voice, "*Hmm ... Para ti.*"

Seven rays? For me? I wondered why he had said this. I wondered why this sign was here. It would be years, and several hard knocks later, before I would find out.

We were just about out of the train yard when two men in uniform sprung out at us. They had pulled their guns and were aiming them our way.

"Hands up. Now."

Our hands went up.

"No one move."

One of the men held his gun on us while the other went first to Jim and then to Mark to examine their I.D.'s.

Mark engaged them in conversation. "Oh. We didn't know it was illegal. No one told us. They let us get on in L.A. and Texas."

Now my head was pounding, my abdomen was aching, and my nose was running. I reached into the pocket of Mark's coat, which I was still wearing, to get a handkerchief. The officer with the gun pulled lurched toward me. I thought he would shoot. My hands went higher into the air as I shouted a "No!"

The uniformed men both looked at me, surprised. The one with a gun reached over and pulled off my hat. My hair came tumbling down. "Bill. She's a girl. Damn."

"Well, my oh my. A girl in the yard. And just a kid, too."

He reached over and put his hand in my pocket. All he found to pull out was the handkerchief. No gun. He checked the other pocket and then he felt me up and down far too thoroughly. "She's clean."

"How old are you?" the other one demanded.

"Nineteen."

"Oh yeah? She looks like jail bait to me."

"Prove it. Got some I.D.?"

I reached down with both hands to pull my license out of my sock. The armed man held the gun right up next to my hands. I froze. He put his own hand in my sock and found the card.

They read it together and found that I was indeed just now nineteen. "Hey look at this photo, Bill. She don't look so bad all cleaned up." He leered at me.

"Yeah. She's a real cute honey."

The sun abruptly dropped below the horizon and left us in a chilly darkness. I chanted a prayer again, wondering if the rainbow of Seven rays still floated above us. But I didn't dare look away from the gun.

Eventually they focused on the brown gnome-man. He had I.D., too. Only it was a voter registration from Baja, California.

"Baja?" the man with the gun on us asked.

"Where's that? Anyone know where that is?" the other one demanded.

"Baja means southern," Mark informed them.

"Actually it means lower. That's like southern." I tried to sound helpful.

31

"Lower?"

"Yeah Bill, that means he's from southern California, not Mexico."

"Shit, I know that. Think I'm an idiot or something?"

"Well anyway, you kids're damn lucky we aren't arresting you. But we've got something worse in store for you. We're kicking you out of the yard and making you walk to the bus station through angry East St. Louis on election night. We're having about eleven murders a day there right now. You'll wish we'd put you in jail."

"Now get out of here."

We left the yard and headed through town – East St. Louis on election night – to the bus station. It was the longest walk we ever took. We said very little to each other, being more concerned with safety than conversation. Asking directions wasn't easy. Most of the people we talked to didn't want to answer us. We could feel the tension in the air as we traipsed through it. We could hear windows breaking and people yelling. We thought we heard a few gunshots followed by screams.

Just as it became clear to us we were entirely lost, as we were coming around yet another desperately dark corner in a very run down area, a tall black man in a sort of African robe and hat appeared before us. His exotic colorful attire jumped out of the dark dingy setting and stunned us. He must have been coming around the corner from the other direction, I told myself to explain his sudden appearance. He stood in front of us, his arms folded and said, "Uh, uh."

We stopped walking and faced him speechlessly. What had we gotten ourselves into now, my mind asked itself as it raced through the recent months of danger and discovery.

The tall black man eyed me. "Man, dey kill ya' 'f'ya' go dere."

In spite of my warnings to myself, I retorted quietly, "Well then, which way should we go? All we want to do is get to the bus station. You think people would tell us how to do that."

"Thatz 'cross de rivah. Ya' won't make it, lay-dee."

Mark decided to participate in the conversation. "Why?"

"Dey kill foolz, mahn."

"Why?" Mark asked, sincerely curiously.

"Ya' be foolz ta' cross dis place, dis iz a pit, mahn."

"Then help us," I said, practically pleading that he do so.

"Wat'ya got ta trade, womahn?"

"Nothing," I ventured, "we gave what we had to this man who's trying to get to Chicago."

"Do ya' come here from de yahd?"

"We got kicked out of the train yards if that's what you mean."

He looked at each of us, his eyes finally landing on the gnome-like man. They eyed each other for a while, exchanging no words, but ending with a small mutual nod of some form of acknowledgement quite foreign to me.

Now the tall black man shifted his attitude and changed his style of speech. "All right kids," he said, "look, this is no place for people like you, especially a girl. I'll walk you out. It's a long way and

I don' wanna' heya cumplainin.' Do you understand? You'd better because I'm the only help you'll get around here."

He looked at Mark.

"Yep," Mark answered.

He looked at Jim.

"Yes."

He looked at me, studying my face for an answer as to why on Earth I would be there on that street on that night with these people looking the way I did and being so obviously ill.

I could tell he was wondering all this, but all I said was, "Sure and thank you."

The black man looked at the gnome who nodded a yes, and then he and the black man headed up the street together. They looked so odd up in front of us, one so tall and the other so short. And from such different worlds. They seemed to be having a conversation, but I wasn't sure what language they were speaking.

At one very wrecked part of town, the two of them seemed to decide to protect us from the back as well as the front. The tall black man went to the rear of the pack, and the gnome-man beckoned me to walk up front with him.

He and I didn't talk much. In fact, all I really did was listen to a few of his utterances when I could make them out. He sounded like he was speaking a very old language. At one point he turned to me and said in Spanish, "*Mire, las siete rayes*," look, the Seven rays, and waved at the sky.

I looked up. There were no rainbows. It was the middle of the night. *"Pero, no hay nada, no hay nunca de sus luces."* But there is nothing, there are none of your lights, I told him.

He stopped, took my hand the way Kiowa once had, and pointed it to the same constellation of the Seven sisters that Kiowa had shown me. Needless to say, I was surprised.

"Las siete estrelles de las siete rayes."

The Seven stars of the Seven rays? I looked at the gnome-man incredulously.

All he did was nod gravely and add, *"Es la puerta."*

Okay, fine. He's telling me this is the door. The door? The doorway? To what exactly? I mulled this mystery over until we reached the bus station while he chanted under his breath.

After we bought him a ticket, we got my most recent contact with the spirit world, this gnome-man, safely onto the bus to Chicago. As he was climbing onto the bus, I wanted to thank this man, but didn't know how. He seemed to know this, turned to me, and said, *"Circa Uxmal. Una sonote. La puerta."*

"What?" I forgot myself and asked in English. What was Uxmal? What was a *cenote*? The doorway?

All he said was, *"Quetzalquato, pajaro de las rayes."*

What was that word? Kayt-zahlz-kwah-toe? The bird of the rays?

I had no idea what he meant and would not know for quite some time. But I determined I would one day find out the meaning of his departing puzzle.

We waved goodbye. When we turned around, our black guide was also gone. After searching for him a while and not finding him or anyone who had seen him even though he was so tall and colorfully dressed, the three of us, Fire Star Tribe refugees, hitchhiked out of town and finished our trip.

And, I never saw the gnome-man again, even though he had helped me in a time of great crisis – he had called the spirits in to save my life. He had left us with an address in Chicago to write. My later letters to him were always returned "no such person at this address." I kept thinking maybe he wasn't really a person, but I didn't know what this might mean. I knew he held a key to the door of the locked spirit realm. I knew the Seven-rayed rainbow sign he had shown me was a clue, but I couldn't figure out what to do with it. Maybe my gnome friend would find me again. I waited. And waited. And waited some more, on into my life.

Time went by. I began to heal from the miscarriage, but not from the wound in my reality left by the rape at my entry into the Fire Star Tribe. Not from the confusing heartbreak of one's hero gone sour. Fire Star continued to haunt me. I kept seeing his face and feeling his paw-like hands on me. He had told me that there would be nowhere I could go without him finding me. I believed him. He seemed to have that kind of power. And I knew I had to find the Seven ancient spirits, my star family, again – they would help me drive off the Fire Star. But what did he want? What was he after? Why wouldn't he leave me alone?

I kept banging on the walls of this modern white reality, looking for a safe portal to that elusive ancient world. My daily life became a constant pilgrimage toward something I was hard pressed to define: the hazy but crystal clear place I had come to call the spirit realm. I had decided that access to it was my birthright.

More than my birthright. My home. This was the emerging truth, obscure but plain.

Volume Two: Maka Shan Saga

3.
doorways home

We were riding the wave of our times.

Not long after this trip, Mark and Jim and I parted ways. They had to deal with the fact that they were being drafted to serve in the Viet Nam war. I had to try to heal my life, and while I was at it I was determined to gain independent access to the spirit realm. Jim was drafted and went to Viet Nam. Mark went to Paris as a conscientious objector to the war, where he worked for years. I moved on in search, search of something.

I was not ready for the anti Viet Nam War sentiment that seemed to have cycled to a new peak while I had lived with the Tribe and then had traveled the US by freight train. Now, there I was right in the middle of it, in Berkeley California, quite by chance. I had come in search of an old childhood friend, Gabriel, of Native American descent, who had expected to, about now, be a student at the grand old University of California at Berkeley. But I could not find him. I wanted him to explain to me all that I could make no sense of, but clearly he was not to be found. I did manage to find someone, amidst the riotous mass on campus, who knew who Gabriel was. I was shocked to hear that Gabriel had been drafted, especially since he had been an anti-war organizer. His lottery number had been called and that was that.

What times these were. The United States appeared on the verge of its own civil war, and I was not alone in my spiritual and cultural confusion. It was as if many different energies far larger than we were were playing out some kind of struggle through us. Later, eventually, many of us would have children and perhaps try not to tell them everything about what we had been through. But the world would know anyway.

This day back then, flames spiked at the center of the riotous mass as, one by one, protesters, dressed in torn second hand army fatigues, tossed their burning draft and draft lottery cards into cans usually reserved for refuse. Shouts of "Stop the killing! Stop the killing!" came from various corners of the mob. One angry protester dressed in military garb climbed onto the stage and began screaming "They're killing children too!" A policeman tried to stop the protester but could not. The crowd cheered him on. Someone else yelled, "And we red men are out there dying first! Native American cannon fodder!" I was scared for my friend Gabriel as I recalled my friend Kiowa's reports of his own experience in the Southeast Asian jungle trenches. So many Native Americans who had served in "Nam" had collected up on that Fire Star tribal land. They had gone there in search of something, like I had.

Just then, from one moment to the next, there was a profound surge of activity and the protesters, the police, and all were swallowed by rushing people. Fires flared as cans of burning draft cards were spilling and other items were being thrown onto the flames. The body of swarming humans, now more an animal of one mind, began to move down the street, marching rapidly on the verge of full stampede, toward a nearby Army office.

I struggled to make my way out of the chaos and, finally, stood way off to the side, wondering where to go and what to do next. It seemed I had no place there or anywhere else for that matter. I felt so lost.

And then I remembered my planetary home – the one most people think of as actual home. Yes, home, where I had a parent and a sibling. This was home enough for now, at least it would be for an hour or two while I determined the next step in my confusing journey. In that instant, I felt as drawn to the place as I had to anywhere else ever.

****

And so it was that early one evening a few days later, grimy, skinny, holes in my clothes, my long hair wild, I walked into my father's home. I did my best to act nonchalantly, as if nothing at all had happened and no time had passed, and as if I wasn't still being stalked by the spirit of Fire Star. What Fire Star wanted from me, I still could not see.

First, I stood quietly outside the front door for a few minutes, stuffing my pain, mastering my confusion, and mustering up the guts to face the family. Then I forced my feet to walk me into the house. My heart began pounding as I opened the door, which greeted me with a squeak, just as it used to do when I'd snuck in after the family curfew.

I faced the door as I pressed it closed, careful to make no more sound. I stood just inside and looked around, shocked to find that everything looked different. Could this be the place where I had grown up? Nothing had been moved, nothing had been touched since my mother had died, but nothing at all was the same. Memories rattled around in my head. That was my mother's favorite chair. That was where my father always sat facing my mother. That was the warrior vase my grandfather had brought back from China so long ago.

I shivered suddenly – I felt a threatening tug on my inner composure. Just when I needed all my power to deal with coming to this home again, something from the non-physical world, something that was part of Fire Star, was grabbing at me. Sure, it was the still-raw memory of what that man had done to me. Sure, it was a little of what psychologists would later come to call post-traumatic stress disorder. And it was far more. He was indeed stalking me, following me on some invisible level. He wanted something, wanted something back, it seemed. But what had I taken? What? What? What? I still had no understanding of the transfer of power matters that were driving him. This would become increasingly clear to me during the journey that lay ahead. Funny thing though, every time I would think this matter was finally clear, there would be more to learn about it.

I was determined not to tell my father anything about all that. I waited in the hall until I felt I could focus on what was in the material world right around me rather than on these bizarre sensations and visions. Then I walked down the hall toward my father's voice. On my left, I caught my reflection in the mirror. I had to muffle a gasp. This couldn't be me! I was thoroughly appalled and rejected myself. That wasn't me. I was someone else. I didn't look like that girl. I told myself, do not look again. Not now.

I glanced ahead into the kitchen and saw a sign on the dishwasher saying "dishwasher has NOT been run." That was new. Some paint was cracking in the corner of the ceiling. That was new. There was a white curtain covering the kitchen window. That was new. I stepped out of the dark hallway into the light.

My father and brother were eating dinner. I forced the relentlessly lingering image of Fire Star out of my mind and struggled to find some kind of greeting that would disguise my distress.

"I see you've learned to cook," I said off-handedly, plopping my shabby backpack down in the middle of the floor.

My father and younger brother looked up, stunned. They stared in shock as if I were an apparition or something equally disturbing. A wave of indignation at their reaction came over me, but it was stilled when I realized what they were seeing: the girl in the mirror – this ragged vagabond, damaged, polluted by rape and all the rest.

I felt naked and despicable before them. Can they see his paws on me? Will they guess what happened? No, I told myself, relax. It's just that I look disgustingly awful, and I didn't say I was coming, and I've been missing a while.

"Eeeoooo, look at you, you're disgusting!" my younger teenage brother blurted out. "Where've you been? Dad was so wor—"

My father reached over and put his hand firmly on my kid brother's arm, causing the dear boy to stop haranguing me. Now my brother's expression crashed. I could see he'd been scared I was dead or something. I wanted to tell him I was so sorry, but I couldn't find a way. Again, I got hit with the memory of how close I'd actually come to being killed. Standing there, I could feel Fire Star's hands on my neck, and my throat contracted. I could hardly breathe. Drums started pounding in my ears.

My father just looked at me, smiled as if everything was normal, and said, "You hungry?"

"Um, yep," I replied – relieved, although I was definitely not hungry.

"Well," my brother went on, "I'm glad to see you anyway."

"Well, sit down, relax, you're home," my father said, again speaking up to soothe me. And I did. Strangely, as soon as I sat in the chair – the chair that had been my mother's – the strange drum beat I'd been hearing faded and so did Fire Star.

I tried to stay mentally organized. I kept trying to look like I was focusing on what was going on at the table. "Nice of you to check in every few years," my brother went on, trying to joke. I rolled my eyes at him but I was grateful to him. His words pulled me back to the here and now.

My father ignored my brother's jibes, getting up and serving me some food, while launching into an explanation of the experiments in cooking that he'd been undertaking recently (since my mother's death). He was cutting every vegetable he could find into fine slices and stir-frying the slices together in the Chinese cooking wok I had once bought him. I looked at the stuff he was putting on my plate. It was wild. It had flowers and nuts and strange pieces of things I'd never seen before.

"Eat it, skinny," my brother said. "Where've you been staying? Out with the hobos?"

I glanced at him, nervously, as if he could see right into my recent past. But he was again just joking, nervous at having me home looking like I was looking.

"You leave her alone," my father said to him quietly, as he put a scoop of mushrooms covered in some kind of unidentifiable green sauce smelling like organic fertilizer on my plate.

My brother laughed at the "health" food. My father chuckled. It seemed to be a joke of theirs. My father threatened to serve my brother some of the green sauce.

"Oops, gotta' go, desperate need for a burger. Back soon," my brother said, looking at his watch as he got up. He looked at me, a flood of emotions in his eyes suddenly. "See ya' later, sis, huh?"

"Sure – well, no, I don't know, maybe," I nodded. I was making no commitments, not in the condition I was in. He eyed me. My heart suddenly leapt into my throat as I felt my deep connection with him. And then I felt my mind make the very leap backward that I realized I was so fearing – to my mother, and her death.

After my brother was gone from the room, my father and I just sat there quietly, not talking, not doing anything. I could sense his love for me radiating outward and filling the room, and I could feel him giving me my freedom just to be. I got tears in my eyes. "Dad," I said, putting down my fork, unable to eat even one mouthful of food. "I'm just not hungry. It's good that you're cooking, really. I hope it doesn't hurt your feelings if I don't eat right now."

"You look half starved," he said.

"I'm okay."

"You should have phoned, I would have helped."

"Dad, I said, I'm okay. And I'm sorry. Real sorry."

"All right. Don't worry about it."

I heard my brother trying not to slam the door on his hurried way out. I mustered my strength and took a few bites of the concoction on my plate. It was surprisingly delicious, but I pushed my plate away. "It's great, really amazingly good. Later maybe."

Silence came over us again. My father was giving me my space, not wanting to intrude on me – probably seeing how delicate my emotions were just then. And to make matters worse, the drums in my head started again. Louder and louder. And spirits in the air –

For a brief moment, my father seemed to notice something. He squinted. He studied the air around the room with a strange distant look on his face, as if he was remembering something, as if he had seen something, as if he heard the drums, too.

"What is it, Dad?"

He looked me in the eye. "I just thought I heard something … I don't know … could be my old ears." He squinted at me as if I would have an explanation for what he'd picked up.

"Dad, why are you looking at me like that?"

"Maybe … maybe you can tell me. I … I … I guess you're finished with that stuff on your plate, huh?"

I nodded yes.

He moved the plate away from me. "I was just trying to feed you. After all, what are fathers for?"

I shrugged.

He looked at me sympathetically. "You've lost a lot of weight. Far too much."

"Dad," I said, "don't worry about me. I don't need that. Please."

The drumbeat rose to a deafening level in my mind. I put out a tiny call to Kiowa from a tiny but infinite place very deep within my heart. I heard the sound of rushing water coming closer and closer. The rushing sound filled me through and through, drowning out the drums. Then came the sound of Kiowa's voice in the middle of the rushing water – singing that old, old star song, the one I had recognized that night he had guided me to the spirit realm.

I couldn't help it; tears rushed to my eyes. I looked right down at the table and tried to blink them back. The whole world became a blur. Not knowing what else to do, I started humming the song behind my shut lips. That soothed me inside.

"Beautiful melody. Where did you learn that?" my mildly startled father asked.

I didn't answer and stopped humming, a little embarrassed. Seeing that I was crying, Dad reached across the table and touched my hand. "Hey ..." he said, searching for the right words.

I looked up through my liquid eyes and met his blazing blue ones, which were now filling with tears as well. "Dad, what about you? Are you okay?"

He reflected inward a moment, into his own world, then looked at me again and nodded a solemn yes. "We haven't heard from you in such a very long time."

I shrugged and then stared at his face. I could see it for the first time. He had looked through the agony of grief into the sacred. His eyes were softened more than ever by the loss of my mother in the physical realm.

Walls made of air dropped away and I looked right through space deep into him. I realized that never once in my life had I heard him raise his voice. It would be two decades later before I would finally hear my beloved father shout at me, when he was on his own death bed, begging me to commit euthanasia, trying to convince me he indeed was entirely ready to die – to cross over – to move on through the veil and join my mother in the spirit realm.

But, back then, on this night, I was only nineteen, he was only forty-four. We must have stared into each other's eyes five, ten minutes, I don't know how long. I was finally seeing my father for who he really was – someone just as deep into the spirit world as I was

… deeper even. I don't know how I could have missed seeing my father's wisdom for so many years. I didn't know what I should say to this dear beautiful quiet sage of a man – this white world mystic, now that I could see him?

I realized that his hair had turned entirely white while I was gone. And he is only forty-four, which is not so old, I told myself. I shifted in my chair uncomfortably. The guilt was making me ache – my disappearance had aged him. I guess he sensed me noticing how he'd aged. He tilted his head almost apologetically. "Well, it's a lot for a parent."

A knife hit my heart. "I know Dad. I'm sorry. I just got lost for a while. It just was how it was. With Mom gone …."

The thought of her made me involuntarily press my hands into my abdomen where vague remaining pains were reminding me of the difficult miscarriage in captivity I had suffered. Should I tell him? Why should I hurt him by telling him? How does a girl tell her father she's been raped? And then held hostage for the delivery of the rapist's baby? And that the rapist was, or at least said he was, a medicine man ….

My father looked at me and smiled gently. "Most other fathers would have gone mad by now. Or at least called the police or a runaway office or something. I've done my best to give you your freedom."

I knew he wanted to know what had happened to me. But he didn't need all these ugly pictures in his head. Especially not after my mother's grueling illness and death. Yet, he hadn't deserved my silence – even though my silence was caused by my captivity and then by my shame -- and he had a right to know where I'd been. Didn't he? What was the right thing to do here?

It all made no sense to me, but one thing was for certain. Time right then felt very strange, as if I'd been gone forever, and at the same time had left just yesterday. In the midst of this sensation, I could still hear Kiowa's singing. I started to hum along under my breath again. I couldn't help it.

My father swallowed some more of his green concoction. "Well you just relax. I know you … you and I spent so many, many hours and years together, preparing for this time in your life. And I guess in mine, too. Your mother's sickness and death … that was a great ordeal … for all of us. And I must tell you, somehow, for her and for me, it was a major initiation."

He paused and looked at me closely. "You do know what I mean by initiation, don't you?"

He peered at me, and a quizzical smile appeared in his eyes. The drumming stopped. I nodded a faint yes. Oh boy, did I know what initiation was. Uncertain that I could look into my father's eyes just then without him seeing everything, I started arranging my napkin, knife and fork. Should I tell this father of mine about all that had happened to me – about my anguish and consequent search for the spirit world? He had a right to know.

He was speaking again. "The veil between the material plane, you see, and other realms, that veil opened as your mother was dying. And it is still open, to us. You know what I mean?"

I met his eyes with surprise. "Yes, I think I do."

I looked into those blue eyes of his, those blue flame eyes. What? Oh yes, right. Those eyes! Right! They were carrying the same blue flame as Kiowa's eyes! I caught the vague image of Kiowa flickering into the room in the space behind my father.

"What's that you have?" my father asked, pointing to Kiowa's little white leather blue and ivory beaded bag hanging around my neck. His eyes expressed a momentary recognition. They grew very wide as he stared at the medicine bag. Could he feel Kiowa's presence?

I took a deep breath. I touched the medicine bag. "This? A Native American man, he gave it to me."

Kiowa's image moved in right behind my father. I looked at Kiowa in unabashed awe, and then I caught myself. I adjusted my gaze in a pseudo-casual way onto the face of my beloved father.

I saw my father see me do this. He caught my eye and locked gazes with me. Now time stopped, as I had witnessed it doing elsewhere, right there at the dinner table. There I was, stripped down before the man that had raised me – stripped raw – a world of truth in my eyes – a universe of truth in his. It was an intensely intimate moment – the sort not expected of fathers and daughters. I really had no secrets to tell. This father of mine already knew it all. And although he seemed to accept me and everything I had done, whether he knew the details or not, a more wretched wave of guilt washed through me.

"Dad, I'm really sorry if you've been worried. But … well you see, I—"

"Don't be sorry," he interrupted.

"But what I'm sorry for, is that I'm … leaving again. I have to," I said. And then I paused, catching myself about to speak the truth that was suddenly dawning upon me: I had to get out of this house and right now, because if I didn't, I would be overwhelmed. By my mother, my mother's ghost, something in the air in this house that was so vast, so overwhelming, that I just couldn't open to it – not yet at least.

"I just have to move on, Dad. I don't feel I can do anything but keep on moving right now. I can't hold still, I just came by to let you know I'm doing good, real good deep down. But I'm looking for something … some meaning. Some answers."

He looked casually surprised, but only even that for a moment. "Yes, I know. It's these times … these times we're moving into, they've opened the search up to the people … opened the long hidden Mysteries to all who would honestly wonder." He scratched his head and went on, "The only way to raise a kid like you, a spirit like yours, in these times, is to trust, the way your mom and I did, in the greater guidance."

I raised my eyebrows. To what? The way he and my mother had done what?

He just went right on, "I know I've really done my job. So, you'll be okay. You'll have to be okay. You just go ahead – I trust in the spirits that guide us. I always told myself that when the little bird leaves the nest, you have to know it can fly."

I swallowed, reached without thinking and took his hand, wanting to be sure he was reassured, even if I wasn't. "I can fly, Dad."

"I know." He looked at me with those blue, blue eyes, the color of sky, the kind of eyes you can ride into the cosmos. I knew I would never forget those eyes. Never.

"You taught me to … to fly." I tried to swallow the lump in my throat. I struggled with something I couldn't define as I tried to remain in my seat.

"Well then, I know you'll like what I made for dessert." He laughed and got up to get something from the kitchen while I sat there, more and more agitated, feeling the air in this place where I'd grown up pressing in on me, memories that I wasn't willing, not yet, to be even slightly touched by. "Oh, by the way, there were some men in suits looking for you."

What? What could they want, I worried. … When my father came back to the table, I had to tell him again that I was leaving. "Dad, it's just that I can't be in this house very long."

"Memories?" my father said quietly. "Or the men in suits?"

"No, just the memories. How do you do it?" I had to ask him. Of course, I wasn't being totally accurate. These men in suits, who ever they were, what ever they wanted, were a sort of nagging reality I could not quite make sense of. And they scared me. Friends had left several messages with each other, hoping I would hear from one of them, that men in suits were calling on people I knew, looking for me.

"She's not gone … she's not dead. She's here with us. We live with her."

"But I can't be this close to what happened to Mom, her screaming in pain. I can't, even if her suffering turned this place for you into the doorway to heaven. It's not mine … and I've got to keep on looking."

"That's fine, go then. I will miss you, that's for sure, but I know you need to do your thing. I know you, you've always knocked on that door, pushed that envelope. You know something's out there, you've been in touch, since you were a kid."

"Dad," I swallowed. "I've got to tell you – I've seen them again … my other parents. Remember, those same ones I told you about when I was little?" I looked at him with a wistful excitement. I was sad but happy. I wanted to share this with him but I didn't want to hurt him or make him feel less special to me.

He was serving some kind of purple dessert. Ground berries with some kind of yogurt of something? He grinned. "Thought so."

"There're Seven of them. They speak to me in unison."

"Figured as much."

Really? He figured as much? I cleared my throat. "And, Dad, … I … I …"

"You what?"

"Well, I saw Mom again, too. She was very old this time … a sort of gypsy vagabond priestess or something."

Under his breath, he said, "Sveeka."

I grabbed the edge of the table. "What?" How could he know this name?

"You heard me," he said quietly.

54

At that moment, my brother rushed in with two other gangly teenage boys who were bound and determined to rummage through the refrigerator for whatever hints of normal food they could find. They grabbed three containers of ice cream, some spoons and bowls, sat down at the table.

I was about to get mad at their rudeness when my father caught my eye, winked, and shook his head no.

"Hey thanks, Dad, for remembering the ice cream," my brother said. "Normal stuff."

"Hey, what are fathers for?" he said.

I stood up abruptly. The boys ignored me. My father raised his eyebrows at me, but said nothing. I took Kiowa's white leather medicine bag from around my neck and hung it around my father's neck. "Keep this for me until I get back. Special medicine. Gotta' go."

He put his hand on my arm and leaned toward me. "Special medicine? Have you ever thought that maybe you just might find exactly what you're looking for, right here," he whispered into my ear. "There are things about your roots I have to tell you."

Later, Dad. "I have to find this stuff my way," I whispered under the din of the boys. "Please be all right."

He closed his hand around the bag, and said, "It seems you are already finding these things out."

"It seems." I paused, realizing he had just touched a long agitated nerve. I swallowed. Finally we're going to deal with this, I told myself. "So what percent, Dad?"

"I don't know exactly. Your paternal grandmother. Although it may be more, because of other relatives, I'm not sure."

"Really?"

"Yes."

"Well that's just – "

"A fraction, but I guess the blood runs strong." He finished my sentence.

"Sure seems to," I agreed.

My father and I were silent a moment.

And then suddenly I was irritated. "Wait a minute, Dad. Why didn't you tell me this long ago? I mean, you sure hinted at it a lot, but we never just put it out there."

"I wanted to, but it got lost in the shuffle and really didn't seem relevant to our lives."

"Not relevant? How on Earth can that be true?"

"It just wasn't anything any one wanted to know." My father looked down, almost ashamed for a second.

"How can that be?"

"Your mother and I were worried about the prejudice you kids might face. We had seen enough of it in our lives already and wouldn't have willed it upon you."

"Oh."

"Really."

"Oh."

"And why didn't I get a name that fit my heritage then? Why this Lilith thing? I can't stand this name."

My father was visibly pained by this pronouncement of mine. "Well, your mother – it was important to your mother."

I looked surprised by his pain.

He went on, "She felt it was your heritage in a way far larger than I can explain quickly. She also told me many times that someday you would understand why this strange name. She thought of this as a legacy she was leaving you."

"A legacy?" This made no sense to me.

"Anyway, with all the heritages you inherited, you were up for more than one name."

"I just wish someone had explained things a bit more."

"We figured you would find out on your own if you were meant to know. … As you have and are." My father gazed deep into my soul. "You would find out on your own and then ask the questions to get the answers you needed when you needed them." He studied my face. "Hope this was not too bad an idea."

I gazed back at my father, nervously now. He seemed to be seeing in my eyes the whole thing I had just lived through as it raced again through my consciousness. I was afraid to tell him about it. I desperately wanted to, but I simply could not. So I kept quiet.

He blinked as if to clear his mind's eye, and then nodded a solemn yes. "All right," he told me, "go fly through star fields, reconnect with the ancients, your ancestors. Do your thing. You will see the way, and your mother I am certain will help you. Check back in when you land. Do you need anything?"

I patted my brother on the head, felt my heart reach out to him, denied my heart's longings – and left, as quietly and quickly as I could, grabbing my shabby back pack and flying out the front door with waves of tears in my eyes. I could feel my mother, Sveeka, standing there in the doorway, seeing me off, but I didn't turn back. I just couldn't. My heart was bursting with more feeling than I could handle.

4.
drum beats

Still.

Still I felt the penetrating eyes of Sveeka upon me, as I turned a street corner and headed on away through the night. I felt with eerie certainty that she knew where I was going, what I was seeing, and why. Well, I said to myself, this made some sense, because she was dead. Funny. But what about my father? He knew it all too, and he was on this side of the great divide, wasn't he? My parents unveiled their esoteric realities slowly, over the years of my life. Most of the unveiling actually took place following their respective passings. For now, I was largely on my own. Or so I thought.

I made my way toward the bus stop, through what I still believed was the land of paper people and dead ground – through the neighborhood where I had spent so many years. There were kids' bicycles and baseball gloves left on street corners, a broken doll on a front lawn, a grubby tennis shoe sopping wet in the rain of an automatic sprinkler, and living room windows where the glow of television had everybody hypnotized into being robots. But in the middle of my rejection of this Americana suburban life, I had to admit there were at least glimmers of wisdom hidden there, everywhere. I had seen it in my father's eyes. There were doorways even in this world, openings to the spirit realm. Maybe even big doorways, huge portals, I didn't know.

At each successive street corner, with a steadily building pressure, more and more fragments of memory started being triggered and then unfolding within me. It was as if I was walking through and into the pictures I was seeing. Somewhere in a distant dimension, the drumbeats of the Tribe began again. I feared Star Fire was approaching.

And then, as if in response, or for my protection, the whirling wind I knew Sveeka to ride appeared. "Oh, God," I began mumbling as I walked. "I can't take all this, and now, here is my own mother who was alive in this suburb just a year ago. How can it be? Momma! You were just so terribly degenerating and wasting away. How can you be this magical ancient priestess now?" I was terribly confused by all this, whether imaginary or actual, or something else far greater, or far more mundane.

The drum beats in my mind grew louder. Oh no. Not again. Not now. I pressed my hands to my ears – just as I tripped over something. A sudden gust of a heavier wind whirled up around me and the image of my withered mother as she looked shortly before her death was there before my eyes – one of the memories I was running so urgently away from. It reached through the thin veil and grabbed me. I almost physically stepped through some sort of thin membrane back in time to a little over a year ago – and there I was again, remembering how I had gotten home and found her alone, sitting in the dark just past sunset. I had found her sitting up in her bed, leaning forward, looking into nothingness so intently it scared me.

"Mom," I had whispered as I inched into her bedroom. At first she hadn't heard me. I got closer and saw her pushing with her fingers on something invisible. She was pressing into it with what seemed to be all her weakened might. For an instant, I knew she was pressing against the night, trying to keep it from rolling in.

"Mommy," I whispered, "what are you doing?"

She blinked, turned to me blankly, and leaned back. "Trying not to die quite yet," she told me in a matter-of-fact way.

I remembered the dull agony of this simple but mortifying exchange. I remembered being unsure whether I felt more mystified, horrified, terrified, or just plain heartbroken, but whatever I felt, I dulled the intensity of the emotion in order to cope with the reality I faced – and my mother faced.

As I reviewed this memory, its beauty became clear to me. But I wanted to leave that picture, to avoid it again. I pushed it all back again, depositing the memory deep into my heart. That scene of my dying mother pressing up against the membrane between here and the other dimension faded until all I could see were her eyes looking at me.

The nagging drumbeats, which I had forgotten for a few minutes, were still there, in my head. Now they were too loud. Feeling an inexplicable panic, I started to run. I ran from the drums, from Sveeka, from sadness and loss, from … I wasn't exactly certain what I was running from.

I knew Sveeka was coming after me. And then, I felt Sveeka tap me on the shoulder – but I didn't turn around. I heard a voice echo within me, saying something important. Voices, I should say. And I knew what was happening. It was the Seven, right there, following me down the street of the neighborhood where I grew up. I was in an altered state, *wakan* for some reason, walking quickly – actually jogging now – down the street, talking to the Voices, mumbling to them. I had come to know this *wakan* state perhaps during my childhood, however it was not made clear to me until members of the Tribe I had recently lived with had pointed it out.

Being *wakan* is being in a state of mind where the walls between worlds or realms are for us down, or where we can see through these walls. When one is *wakan*, the view from the physical realm into the spirit realm is pretty good. And one can become better and better at achieving the *wakan* state. This state is not specifically a drug-related state, although there are many that claim this state is best achieved via drugs. But this is not true. This state of mind is achieved by learning the keys to this awareness. Many of us actually stumble into this awareness without understanding what we have done.

I became piercingly aware that someone was standing on a front porch watching me under the streetlights. I stopped my awkward walk-run abruptly and tried to act normal – whatever that might be. I'd been talking to myself. Gesturing to no one. Running in the night.

Normal? I had never been normal….

Troubled to say the least, I shook any lurking remnants of the image of my dying mother out of my head, and waved at the anonymous neighbor. She smiled back, tilted her head at me just a bit, and then went inside her home. I saw her shrugging as she did.

I felt so utterly lost just then, all alone on that suburban street that I could no longer call home. I didn't belong there. I wasn't from there. This wasn't my neighborhood, this wasn't even my planet. And not really even my dimension. Why I felt this, what this meant, was not clear to me back then.

I trudged on. I looked at the stars. I wanted with all my heart and soul and will power to go home. That home. In my youthful desperation, I needed someone urgently, someone to be with me, someone who really understood. I needed Kiowa. I needed him to walk with me, to stand by me, to hand me the key to the doorway home. How could he have shown me the key and then taken that key and disappeared? How could he have touched my heart at its very center – and then have left me behind? Kiowa, come back!

I paused and waited for him, fully expecting a miracle, hoping, even expecting to find myself on the very edge of something vast, some great breakthrough.

But no Kiowa now. Why wasn't the magic working here? Why weren't the keys to higher knowledge opening the doors they once unlocked for me elsewhere? Maybe I needed to call the right beings to me: "Please, Seven, come to me! Seven … Seven … Seven!"

No one appeared.

"Gnome-man, where are you?"

No one answered.

"*Mother Earth, take me home.*"

Nothing happened.

"Sveeka?"

I tried to call out her name again but my tongue would not cooperate. Try as I might, I could make no sounds even approaching the sound of her name. My lips would not form anything like the word "Sveeka." I groped in front of me and behind me for the feel of her windy presence. But I found nothing.

No reply.

Just more drums.

Then it hit me so strongly, as if for the first time I was feeling the immensity of my loss.

I want my baby back!

But … no baby. I stopped walking, grabbed my belly and started to weep and sob. As I did this, without any warning except that I was, of course, focused upon his baby, Fire Star's face flickered into my visual field. I cringed, ready to attack him with all my psychic might and stop him once and forever so he'd stop haunting me like this. But how? How? How? And then, it came to me – how to escape at will from him – I suddenly knew to call in the rushing water to transport my consciousness away from his dimensions of power.

Like rushing water, nothing moves. Like rushing water, nothing moves. Like rushing water ….

Sayeth my name, I said to myself, *if thou wouldst travel upon me*. Oh, but of course! If I want to travel on the stream of rushing water, I have to invoke it, I announced to myself jubilantly. *"Rushing water ... rushing water ... rushing water."* I repeated it perhaps a hundred and forty-four times.

The sound of rushing water filled my ears as I called for it, and yes, the sound drowned out the presence of the man that had touched me in such a violating way. Yet, I was thrown way off balance by my successful invocation of the magic of the water. Unnerved, I almost turned and ran home again to my father.

But I did not even so much as look back now. Instead, the insistent wind of time propelled me on.

And so I had no idea I was being followed down the street by an investigator....

5.
stalked

Finally the bus stop.

I sat to collect myself, watching the night fall as I waited for the late bus to take me out of there. I was actually early. I relaxed and closed my eyes a second. Alone again.

"Excuse me young lady." A man's voice interrupted my brief reverie.

I opened my eyes. He was wearing a black over coat. Where had he come from? What was he doing in this suburban neighborhood? Had he followed me? *Me*?

"Excuse me. US Government," he said showing me his official badge and card as he sat down on the bus stop bench, far too near me for my comfort.

I stood up to leave.

"I wouldn't do that, miss. Not right now," he said as his coat fell open a bit and a small gun in a holster was revealed.

I sat back down. "You must have the wrong person, sir," I offered as politely as I could. "I'm no one important." I was nervous.

"No, I know who you are --"

"That's more than I know," I murmured tritely and immediately regretted it.

"I know who you are, young lady. I followed you from your father's house."

"My father's house? My father sent you?"

"No. He doesn't know I'm here."

"I'm sorry sir, but I have no idea what you want with me. I haven't done anything wrong. Am I supposed to be in trouble or something?"

"No, not so far as we know."

"We?"

"The Domestic Terrorism Squad, miss, the US DTS."

"Domestic terrorism? You really are on the wrong track. I don't even know what that is."

"I understand."

"Well then, can I ask what this is about? My bus is coming soon."

"Don't worry, I won't detain you."

"So what is this about then?"

"Well, young lady, I'm sure you are aware that your father lost his top security clearance several months ago?"

"Security clearance? He had that? What is that actually? What does this have to do with me?"

"You were not aware then?"

"No."

"Well then, let me ask you this. What is your relationship with the Native Militia?"

"The what?"

"The Native Militia."

I wondered whether he meant the armed people, the Underground, at least the people the others said were the Underground, who had lived up with the Tribe while I was there. But now I did not ask. All I said was, "Uh, nothing, none. I have no connection to these people whoever they are," I told him (with relative assurance) that I was correct.

"Is your father an American Indian?"

"A Native American? I think you should ask him this."

"But his father, who worked for the US Government, was."

"US Government?"

"Intelligence."

What? "Really you need to ask my father this. I cannot tell you my family history as I was never really told much about it. And I am not sure I need to be talking to you at all. Sir, no offense, but you are a stranger at a bus stop."

"You're not a member of the Native Militia, are you?"

"No. I don't belong to anything. Again, sir, you are a strange man approaching me at night while I am alone in a bus stop."

I watched him make certain his gun was not showing. "Here again is my badge and card, miss." He showed me his I.D. again.

"Thanks, I believe you. I just don't know what you want with me."

"Let me try this. What about the People's Underground?"

I tried not to look anxious. Did this man know about me being up with the Fire Star Tribe where the People's Underground was hiding? "The what?" I asked. I was not going to get into all this, about any People's anything, let alone this group. Anyway, how could I know this was who he was asking about? Anyway, all I knew was what other people had said about them.

"The People's Underground organization, miss."

"Well, ... I've heard of them, sort of, but I have no connection."

"Are you certain of this?"

"Yes. I have no connection. What's this all about?"

"And what about the Great War – what is that? Why is the People's Underground talking about a so-called Great War?" he demanded calmly.

The *Great War*? What was he getting at and how did he know about this? "Oh, well, the Great War, I've heard of it. Lot's of people think it will come someday well into the future."

"Come when?"

"I have no idea."

"Are you sure you have no idea when, young lady?"

"Yes." I truly had no idea, although I wished I knew. I watched my bus approach and stood.

"Where are you heading?"

"To see friends out on the coast."

"The coast? Santa Cruz? Isn't this where you started college before you dropped out?"

"Yes." How much did he know about me and why was he so interested?

"Why did you leave college?"

"It wasn't working for me, I guess."

"Oh, well then, if this is your answer, that's all for now," he said as he shook his head no. He seemed disappointed for some reason.

"For now?

"Yes, we will find you when we have more to ask you."

"Oh. Then can I go?" I asked as I stood and calmly made a move toward the bus. Why on Earth would this guy want to find me again, I wondered.

"Yes. Goodnight."

"Goodnight."

I departed my childhood neighborhood with my heart in my mouth, uncertain as to why. Life can be so strange.

6.
dancing ghosts

Well, it's a pretty big universe out there…

…and easy to lose your way. You can try counting the stars as you pass them and keeping track of the constellations as they present themselves, but it's quite likely you'll lose track if you depend on these things to find your way home. You see, there is no "where" there.

In the end, home is where the heart is. Like many people, I've had to find my way home time and again, traipsing through dark wildernesses of loss, looking for the Light.

Turns out I was never really lost, I was always with me. And, the Seven were always with me, lighting the way. But I certainly didn't see this at the time. I shielded my heart so as to avoid more pain … and so I was blind. You have to find your heart to find your home. In the meantime, everywhere you look you are lost.

In search of the sacred, and the sacred power I sensed I could someday find, I was blind to what greater forces might be directing my every move. Still, somehow, every step of the way, a new piece of the picture unfolded. I was guided by presences whose constant advice I was then still only vaguely aware of.

I found myself making the decision that I would try something conventional. Maybe this would cure me of my confusion and malaise. Maybe this would even further my search. I decided I would try to to go back to college – back to the same college I had dropped out of to join the Fire Star Tribe before even completing the first quarter of my freshman year. I surprised myself, made my way back to this now itself renegade campus, and re-enrolled.

While intensely familiar, this place was not at all the same. I felt like a whole person who'd been shattered into a dismantled mosaic, heading into a now dismantling world. The university at Santa Cruz was, back then, a grand opening in culture. And, at the same time, it was virtually a wound, bleeding new and unsettling ideas, embellished by the desperate pageantry and dreams of the 1960s and early 1970s. Sprawling and decentralized, this coastal mountain-and-meadow school for minds was being described as the "riot proof campus." Yet, you could smell the unrest all around the place. The rampant although generally still invisible unsettling of the modern soul was surfacing there.

And that place was merely mirroring the world of the time. Or, maybe it was mirroring the far more deeply subconscious knowledge of the time, that time which presaged revelations of the increasing competition for and even blocking, locking, of access to the portals.

A revolution was brewing. I could hear the drum beat rising from the ground – these beats maybe even echoes of the future, presaging the future Great War, the global battle to come in the next millennium. The upheaval was massive and profound and was increasingly evident in those years. And, at the University of Santa Cruz back then, no matter how hard the men in charge tried to dress it down, their experiment in learning was getting away from them. The truth about what was happening there registered in the faces of the students and the professors, and wafted through the forests and meadows through which the campus was sprawled. Professors were sleeping with their students. Both students and professors were taking cocaine and LSD. Outdoor classes were sometimes held in the nude. We sat in our classrooms watching our professors attempt to take us to the cutting edge of thought, listening to them dance with their own words, but listening even more attentively to the sound of time passing and irreversible trends being born.

This was such a funny combination for a young woman on a quest. There I was, after all I'd been through, attempting to be a full-time student at a cutting edge University where I studied with some of the leading thinkers of our times, but where I found few if any I could really talk to about the spirit realm and my journeys to and from its domain. Yes, some of the professors there were taking hallucinogenic drugs, and talking of seeing God, but even they who made themselves out to be in touch with the realities beyond this physical world could not hear me when I asked for true guidance regarding the true spirit realm.

I was returning after a rough, raw, almost deadly, and, yes, in some ways inspiring and exhilarating time out in an entirely different world. Nothing about the redwood-studded campus of Santa Cruz looked the same to me after what I had been through. Now, everywhere I looked, I could sense the ongoing invasion of the paper people and the dead ground – camouflaged as a great and very liberal university – working its way into Mother Earth's domain, smothering *Maka*. I admit, my perspective on the entire white world was now very negative. I felt not quite white and, regularly, people on campus were assuming that I carried some of what Fire Star had called red blood. I thought that my face must carry traces of my Fire Star Tribe experience, and that this was why I was being seen as a "breed" as I was being called – a part white, part so-called red person – a cross between races. And, I suppose it might also have been the genetic imprint of a Native American grandmother some generations back. As a result, I came to see and feel acutely, from the inside out, the pervading though often entirely unconscious racial prejudice existing even on this most liberal campus. It wasn't overt or even conscious prejudice. It was subliminal, even subconscious, prejudice against a way of seeing realities.

And so I found it unexpectedly difficult to reintegrate myself into this mainly white college-town world. Not only was I still being pursued by the ghostly presence of Fire Star, not only was I heartsick over the loss of my baby, I was just starving for more positive contact with the spirit realm. And LSD was not the key. No hallucinogen would be the purest key to pure truth.

Half lost in my yearnings for a deeper, real-er, reality, I had to make myself work hard to concentrate intently on what was, supposedly, the education I was trying to get. Yes, I found lodging, and jobs, and I attended classes. I walked through the usual student routines – but a dominant part of me felt entirely separate, not able to dissolve into this everyday student identity at all.

Right at this time in history, quite a large number of returning Viet Nam vets were going to college around the country. At Santa Cruz, this development brought a number of veterans of that disastrous war to the campus and into the classroom alongside their younger, more naive, less world-wizened counterparts. Among these Vets were quite a few Native American men, many of whom had been used as front-line cannon fodder, had seen far too much carnage, and had been hit emotionally and spiritually – just as roughly as had Kiowa.

Kiowa continued to come regularly into my mind, my heart and my dreams. This man had touched me to the absolute quick, and I felt without question that I was his woman – yet, where was he? He had my heart, but meanwhile my body was so alone, wandering around this lonely world waiting for him, waiting for something to open up for me. Meanwhile, I was seriously lost in what, from the outside point of view, must have appeared to be at least a slight state of disoriented depression.

One day, some escape did come. I was wandering down a dirt path through the woods on campus, wondering vaguely why I had walked that way. I was whispering to myself, repeating again with each step, what had become my mantra, my verbal baby blanket: "*like rushing water, nothing moves ... like rushing water, nothing moves.*" I guess I had put myself into somewhat of a trance. I was thankful for the unusual feeling of a relieving lightness in my chest – when, from way off the path, came the sound of someone singing very quietly.

The song, mixed with the sounds of wind sighing and birds whistling high in the towering redwood boughs, was vaguely familiar to my ears. It triggered a sudden wave of nostalgia deep within me. I turned and tried to see who might be singing and where the voice was coming from. I followed the sound of the voice deeper into the woods, far from the rhythms of the paper people located nearby. Finally, lo and behold, there was a man under a tree, kneeling and placing rocks in a circle while he chanted a definitely Native American prayer.

He was in his late twenties, dressed in regular clothes of the times. My guess was that he was a Vet. His beautifully chiseled face looked like he had quite a bit of what Fire Star had called red blood in him. He was tall and strongly built, but at the same time, lean. I guess he felt me watching, because he stopped what he was doing, froze, and stared at the ground.

"Sorry," I said. "*Mitakuye oyasin.*"

He looked up at me then, and narrowed his eyes. "What did you say?"

"*Mitakuye oyasin.* All my relations."

"Oh, you're red, maybe Lakota? No, Cherokee?"

"Who? Me?"

"I see it in your face, the cheeks, the jaw line."

"Some part is, I hear."

"Well, now you know. I'm never wrong about this. I'm a keeper of lineage. So anyway, sit if you like. Pray to spirit with me," the man invited.

I felt a rush of enthusiasm, of hope, of my heart opening and pounding loud with thankfulness. Home, I said, a way home. I sat and crossed my legs just outside of the circle he was forming, and he started to sing again. And, I again recognized the song. At first, I hummed along. Then, where I could, I joined in with the words.

He glanced at me several times during the song, puzzled and obviously pleased. When he was finished with his song, he sat with his eyes closed a moment. Then he opened his eyes and pulled out a pipe – the long-stemmed kind, the Lakota Sioux *Chanupa* I had seen used in pipe ceremony. He lit it and moved it in the directions of the four winds, then looked at me. I extended my hands. At first he hesitated, and then he handed me the pipe. I moved it in the directions of the four winds as well, said a prayer into the sky, took a puff, and passed it back to him. I had learned this ritual up on tribal land.

We silently sat there for about an hour. Part of the time, I was focused only on the nature around me, the power of the Mother Earth, *Maka*. … Then, memories came to me. These were memories of being with the Fire Star Tribe, memories of those deep, deep experiences which weren't part of the white world, which sometimes seemed as if they hadn't happened at all. These memories made me feel crazy because the experiences were so powerful, so wonderful, yes some so painful, a few so wrong, and all so real -- real yet so apparently absent from the outside world.

But, now, these memories marched vividly through me, the song of this man being great validation. I was abruptly grounded and balanced in the depths of the spirit world.

Finally, a bit of healing peace had come to me.

The mystery man, who had unexpectedly given me this gift on my returning to the world that was apparently the "real" world for me, moved out of his own reverie and put his pipe away. I noticed that he left the stone circle as he had made it. Perhaps he thought he would return to this site, to balance his studies with his ancient ways.

"Thank you for letting me be part of this," I said.

"Can you tell me where you learned of these things – even of the sacred *Chanupa*?"

Just as soon as I opened my mouth to tell him the answer, Fire Star's face came into the space before me. I shook my head, as if to shake the sight of him off. I had thought I'd gotten him out of me for good. "I lived with the Fire Star Tribe," I said simply.

This man who had shared ceremony with me flinched visibly at the mere mention of that name.

"Don't worry, I'm not one of Fire Star's people," I said defensively. But I stiffened as Fire Star's image flickered in and out of my visual field. Go away.

"Hmmm." He studied my face. "I can see that you are not. This is good. You know you can travel the red road without Fire Star."

"But there are some real good people living up there," I added rather tensely. "And some real good teachings going on."

"Yes." He watched me carefully, as if sensing that Fire Star's presence was pressing in upon me. He stood up, lit a branch of an herb, and ceremoniously waved its smoke around me. As he did, Fire Star faded away.

"You are more red than you know," he told me. "Red blood has worked its way into many blood lines now. You are one of us, I can see."

I said nothing.

"Perhaps you would like to come to a secret dance?"

"Oh. What dance?"

He paused, squatted before me a moment, and let his words come to him, I gathered from some deep inner voice. "The ancient Paiute visionary Wavoka, he brought us this dance. He was sick and near dying. Unconscious for days, he crossed over into the spirit realm and made contact with the Great Father who showed him how to bring peace to his people, and to help them coexist with white man. Wavoka awoke and brought the Ghost Dance to all the native tribes – to save them. And," he added gravely, "to bring back those who had died at the hands of white men. To let them cross over and back in."

"Why is it a secret dance?" I wondered aloud.

"To protect it."

"To protect it from what?"

"Well, things like the US Government, for one. Such as the FBI."

"Really, FBI?" I had heard they were looking for me, trying to talk to me again. But I wasn't going to tell this man this. Not right then.

"Oh yes, you see, when Wavoka taught the native people to Ghost Dance, over a hundred years ago, it became very popular and more and more powerful. So, the whites found it a threat, although that's not what it was in the beginning. It was declared an illegal dance by white government. Such idiots. It is simply a dance designed to protect the spirits of the dead, especially the dead warriors, to help them survive the threats to the survival of their spirits. Someday this dance will belong to everyone dancing to survive."

"What do you mean?"

"Mother Earth, she is coming to a *grand metamorphosis*. All of us are going there with her. Maybe even forcing her there. In certain dimensions, she will have to die to survive. So will we. ... So we will dance – dance to protect our souls, and soon the soul of *Maka*, too. Dance is a prayer, it is a meditation, an invocation ... a ceremony direct to Creator. Dance is protection ... especially this dance."

"Is this about the future Great War?"

He looked quite surprised and then nodded a quick yes. "Oh yes, yes. Well, yes, that is, in a very special way, a way you will understand when you see it."

What he said struck a deep chord within me. I knew what he meant. Could we ward off the Great War? Were there enough years left to rewrite the future of this planet? Somehow, I had known the time was coming, known all my life. And it seemed that everywhere I went, news of the coming Great War was coming to me. ... So, I agreed to join him, and to travel with him to this ceremony in the near future. We parted, as quietly as we had come together.

part two:

stalking the portal

7.
spirit writer

It was a long and ongoing remembering.

After that wonderful ceremonial experience with the man in the woods, I found myself yearning even more for a return to the spirit world I'd known with the Fire Star Tribe. Regardless of what had happened to me with Fire Star himself, I remembered vividly the many remarkably positive times up there. There were so many experiences in which I had communed directly and unquestioningly with the spirit world. How could I forget all this, and just let it drift away?

And yes, I still missed my guide and advisor, Kiowa, and even more so now. Every time I called him to me, the sound of rushing water rose within me. I kept expecting him to appear in my physical life, because I felt him so close in to my heart, on deeper dimensions. But still he didn't come to me. My heart cried out, but I remained alone. I repeated and repeated my constant "rushing water" mantra; I found myself saying this under my breath almost continuously. While Kiowa did not appear, this effort sustained me, this inner chant kept me with one foot in the spirit world even as I went through my dry, almost lifeless, robotic everyday paper world activities at work, at home, and at this thing they called college.

Sometimes I felt I needed to find someone, like Kiowa, who could finally break the curse of Fire Star and set me free. Most of the time, well, I just went about my life as best I could, keeping my guard up against Fire Star breaking any more deeply into my consciousness than he already had. Why didn't he get what he wanted from someone else, I kept wondering. Why? And then I would cringe at the thought of this man raping one more girl, one more woman.

In this state, it was hard to come close to anyone around me. Young men wanted my attentions, there was a lot of sexual energy in the college air, but this was not interesting to me then. My sexual feelings were in utter disarray. I was sometimes possessed by deep yearnings for Kiowa. But I met no one on campus who could even begin to understand what was happening inside my heart and mind. No one who I could come close to. What was I to do, where was I to go, to break free of this seeming impasse I was currently stuck in? Why was I here? Why was I white? Or was I?

A happenstance meeting would give me a clue. I had planned to meet a friend at a coffee shop. He was going to be there immediately after a seminar he was taking. As it turned out, that seminar happened to spill over into that coffee shop, as my friend and four or five classmates, along with their professor, took over a table to continue with their discussion.

I sat at the edge of the group, feeling out of place, waiting for them to finish, barely listening, letting the words I heard roll right through me without sticking. Feeling intrusive, I let my long hair fall forward, hiding my face, and looked down. Staring at the table, waiting, I occupied myself with that mantra of mine. *"Like rushing water ...."*

I repeated it under my breath over and over, as I scribbled senseless doodles on a pad of paper.

Then something stopped my hand, and paused my mantra. I looked up. What had I just heard this man say? I was only conscious of the end of his comment: "... careful when walking in two worlds."

The man, the professor who was speaking, caught my eye. I looked at him, wondering why he was at just that moment also looking directly at me. He continued to talk to the group, and make eye contact with the group, but quite artfully, kept returning to his eye contact with me, and didn't let it go.

What the strange professor was talking about now caught my interest most keenly. He was telling the group about how he had been born in Guatemala, where he had grown up with the indigenous peoples of Central America, and formed a deep sense of affinity with them. I studied his face. Yes, there was something foreign to the white world – something I recognized – in that face. There was a particular kind of glint in his eyes, one that told me he knew much more about the ancient realities than he was saying. Had he touched the magic? Had he been through ancient portals? Did he know the spirit realm?

I decided I wanted to meet with this man. This was easily accomplished, as the friend I was waiting for, a young writer, admired this man and continued talking with him after the rest of the group had left the table. The professor sipped at a cup of tea a moment, letting the seminar dust settle before he looked up at me again. He met my eyes, then extending his hand in formal greeting.

As soon as we touched hands, I felt the rhythm of the indigenous within him. Meanwhile he was studying my eyes as if he were a detective. I let him look into my soul, hoping he would see my inner quest, because I had no idea as to how to present my search to him.

My friend, watching this, saw only a long handshake – too long – and a gentle stare down. Having his own designs on me, and wanting to be certain there was nothing amorous in the intense recognition he'd just witnessed, he put his arm around me and began talking to me about this professor.

"This man has spent time with the Omo Lacandon Mayans who still live in the Yucatan Peninsula of Mexico. They're the only arm of the Mayans who were never conquered by the Spaniards and whose leader is the only remaining and thus the last authentic Mayan chief."

"Oh, really?" This professor would therefore definitely have some information for me. "You know the last authentic Mayan chief?"

He answered in a soft voice. "Well, that's what most all of the Indios in Guatemala and the Yucatan say about Old Od Chan K'in."

"Well then, is he a man who can speak directly to the gods?"

The professor looked at me, veiling his surprise as much as he could. "In fact you are exactly right. How come you know about this?"

I wasn't sure what to say. "Oh, well, I've known some Native Americans, in this country. I guess there would be some parallel beliefs and teachings about the true chiefs."

"Yes, in some ways, there are."

I had to know more about old Od Chan K'in. It turned out that this Mayan chief had been known as the Last Lord of Palenque for most of his life, the *T'o'ohil* – Great One. His authority was recognized by all other Mayans because he was the last of the *Halach Winik* – Great Lords – of the whole of the Olmec-Mayan tradition once occupying what is now northern Guatemala and the Yucatan as well as other areas in Mexico.

"They see this era we're living in as the end of the line," the professor explained, "however this might be interpreted. Od Chan K'in does too. He says that, 'When the last Lacandon dies, the world will come to an end.' A hint we all must at least examine, wouldn't you say?"

I thought about this so-called "hint" coming at me all over again, right then and there, and nodded a grave heartfelt yes.

"So you are highly intrigued by the indigenous cultures," Victor said to me quietly.

"Well, yes, especially by what they think of as sacred."

"Hmmm," he studied my eyes again. "And if I might ask – what are you searching for in this material?"

"A bridge."

He watched me very carefully now. "A bridge. A bridge between exactly what and what?"

"A bridge between worlds – neither of which I really fit into."

"Ah yes. It's difficult, isn't it," he said. "I have had to learn this – how to walk in two worlds. You will too, I'm sure."

"I hope so. But I'm not sure how." Maybe he could tell me, I said to myself.

"Well, I will tell you – if you really want to find the bridge, you have to become the bridge yourself. This will take knowing both worlds, the ancient and the modern, very well. It's a lifetime commitment. Two very thorough educations – of equal weight and depth – one balancing the other. Not just this one." He waved his arm as if to encompass the entire white world university system.

I blinked and shook the sound of rushing water out of my mind. I needed to hear with every piece of myself what I was being told here. I knew that this man was speaking right to me, right to the heart of my life.

"It is definitely a lifetime of commitment," he said again, studying my eyes to see if I got it. "Take it from me, when you see the connections between the worlds, you will want to broadcast them. Just remember that you must be careful – subtle – in your presentation of what you see." He studied me a moment and then added, "Especially the more revolutionary parts," with a chuckle.

I nodded another grave yes but probably looked the way I felt, perplexed.

He smiled at me. "Just be careful how you spill the beans. Always remind yourself – *no es un juego, es realidad. Me entiendes*?"

"Always remember that this is not a game, this is reality."

"*Pero, si, claro pues*." But of course, he said. And then it was past time for me to leave and get to my job at the bookstore downtown. The professor seemed ready to go somewhere also. As we shook hands goodbye, he suggested that I "go visit the Mayans," and then winked at me as he whispered, "I am entirely certain they know you. You will see someday why I say this."

"Okay, someday."

"Make a point of it, go to them within the next few years. Start in Guatemala, and whatever you do, don't take a tour guide with you." Victor tilted his head slightly toward my friend, who had momentarily turned to chat with someone at the next table. Then he studied my eyes and nodded. … "Do the important part of your journey alone. This will lead you to your power."

"My power?"

"Yes, it is yours, rightfully yours now."

"I don't understand."

"Oh, but you do. I see this truth in you, and so do you. You just haven't put it all together yet."

I scowled trying to understand this. "Why do I keep hearing things like this?"

"Why does anyone magnetize a certain set of experiences for her or him self?"

I nodded politely as my friend turned back to face us. Then I said my goodbye to both of them and grabbed the next bus, trying to get to work on time. I was intrigued by what this strange teacher who would, many years later, cycle back into my life, had said. He left me feeling the call of indigenous Central America. What a mystery, to be pulling to something so foreign yet so familiar. Why?

8.
host of visions

The day to journey to the Ghost Dance arrived.

I got up early, excited, with a host of visions from Fire Star Tribe ceremonies filling my mind – then met up with the pipe carrier I had found in the woods. He carefully checked his rear view mirror, to be certain we weren't being followed. I found this comforting, as I was, perhaps for different reasons, concerned about the same thing. For days, I had been avoiding the place where I was living in Santa Cruz, having heard from my increasingly suspicious housemates that the FBI or something had been there looking for me several times. I still couldn't quite figure out what they wanted.

The long five-hour ride into the mountains in this old truck reminded me of that parallel pickup journey I had taken not so very long ago, when Gun had transported me to the land where I met the amazing Kiowa, my *Wananeechee* – guide, and was initiated into the realm. I could feel the parallels – however, this time, I knew in my heart that I would stay free. I was no longer the naïve girl who had walked in and been taken by Fire Star; never again would I be anyone's captive, I told myself. I had already paid the price of entry into the realm, a price I should not have had to pay to go there. The knowledge I was coming into was everyone's – was also mine, free to behold. It was our, my, birthright. It was our, my, power, I told myself. Or some voice within me said....

Pipe Carrier, which it turned out was what he actually wanted to be called, and I talked very little during the trip up into the mountains to the east. Instead, we moved again into a serene sort of partnership, silently enjoying the sun's light as it hit the land and made large scapes of color and form.

I must have fallen asleep long before we turned off the highway, onto the long road, into a place with no name, the secret camp. I awoke hearing Pipe Carrier say, "We made it. Thanks to Creator, this old truck carried us here."

I opened my eyes and saw the end of a rugged dirt road leading to a very vague and very narrow footpath into a very thick and virtually impenetrable forest. First, we parked amidst a metallic swarm of some thirty or more old and rusty trucks and cars. Next, Pipe Carrier went to great extremes to be certain we were not being watched. Then, I followed Pipe Carrier a long way through the dark of the forest, finally coming into a stunningly colorful and visually intense scene. We emerged from the thick shade squinting. I saw ahead of me a wide clearing where a large circle had been outlined in unusually red dirt with leaves and sticks.

A group of Native American men wearing the most beautiful hand painted costumes I had ever seen, predominantly deep red, were standing in a tight circle within this larger dirt circle, singing a captivating song to a drummer's beat which maintained the rhythm of a heartbeat: boom BOOM boom BOOM boom BOOM. In the very center of the men was a large cedar tree covered in red ribbons, bones and arrows.

The fifty or more people standing around the circle were moving in time with the songs of those inside the inner circle. The singing men in the circle began to dance, gravely stepping round and round as a group, from right to left. Then the people surrounding them joined in, forming a circle around the singing men, and beginning to sing with them. Some of the outer circle dancers were in blue jeans, the others were in beautiful hand painted costumes of all colors – costumes made of canvas and leather, covered with stripes and shapes of birds – crows, eagles, thunderbirds – also turtles, circles, stars, moons, suns, and lines – lots of lines – with talismans. Several of these dancers, costumed and otherwise, had painted their faces in stark colors with lines and shapes.

Pipe Carrier nudged me. "Those black birds painted on their shirts are crows. Those feathers they are wearing are crows' too. The crow is the sacred bird of this dance. He symbolizes death because he is black. He is the sacred bird that guides the spirits of the dead back from the other world to rejoin the living."

Right then, the butt of a rifle pressed sharply into my side. I thought I heard myself gasp. My heart rate shot up. I gulped in too much air. Menacing memories of rifles up at the Fire Star Tribe pulsed through my system. And Fire Star's rifle.

Pipe Carrier turned as the rifle bearer demanded of him, "What's she doing here?"

"She is with me," he answered sternly.

"What does that mean?" the gunman barked back.

Pipe Carrier made a move, grabbed the rifle butt, and forced it toward the ground. "I say she should be here. She's part Tsalagee, and she is with me."

The rifle bearer backed off. "Well, are you dancing today?"

"No."

"Okay then, but you watch this woman. We don't want any spies. You keep her here for a while and then you take her out of here at night. She should not learn the way."

The rifle bearer stomped off. Pipe Carrier turned to me. "He is no matter. They will dance for five days. We'll stay as long as you want to … you all right?"

"I just don't want any more guns on me," I shuddered. What were they worried about – that I would tell someone how to find this place? That I would tell someone how to Ghost Dance? That I would tell someone that they were Ghost Dancing? I figured it was most likely the last of these, and also a bit of all of these, concerns that kept them on edge. But I was safe, I wasn't a threat, wasn't this obvious? I was safe enough for everyone concerned. For everyone but myself….

We watched as the dancers in the second circle began moving more rapidly around the inner circle of drummers. Some of them were pulled into the center circle by the men there who had started the dance. The two concentric circles were rotating quite intensely now, and in opposite directions.

"Look there. They are making two circles and rotating opposite. This is the special move that makes a strong wave to the center. Look there. The force of opposing directions forms an opening, an energy opening. Look, you see, they are really getting into it now."

I watched as the momentum picked up to a feverish pace. "They're actually generating electricity with this rotating in opposing directions, aren't they?" I said, amazed to see some flashes of energy in the air over their heads. I was soon to realize that they were indeed generating a portal, an opening into the next realm.

"You got it. A special charge is made by this. This is special. No outsiders ever get to see."

I started to say I was not an outsider.

He just put his finger to my lips and said, "I know."

I saw several of the dancers begin shaking as if the current was running right through their bodies. A few broke free of their circles. Now they were pulled toward the center area of the center circle, where they became more furious in their shakes and spasms.

I said, "Oh, wow, what're they doing now?"

"They've gone into trance. Soon some of these people will fall over and become quite stiff. Dead sort of."

We were silent for at least an hour, captivated by our visual feast of all this energy and dancing. Sure enough, at some point, several dancers collapsed in the center of the circles and lay on the ground stiffly. A medicine man who seemed to control what happened in the center watched over them.

"What's going on there?" I asked.

"They're unconscious, in the world of the dead, communing with the dead now."

"They sure look dead," I agreed.

"They are dead for now but they will come back to this life after they travel beyond. Sometimes a hundred people drop over like that. Later they come to and report on what they have seen and learned from the dead."

There were a number of women among the dancers. We saw one of them who had been dancing in the outer circle begin to flail her arms and spin wildly, wailing words in a language I could not understand.

"She's seeing the dead – her dead families – now. They are speaking through her."

The medicine man in the center of the center circle pulled this woman to the center, where she gasped, collapsed to the ground and remained unmoving.

Pipe Carrier started to tell me some history. "You probably know how, during the 1800s, white officials had done all they could to cut the land owned by reds way back. By the end of the 1800s, most of the red nations had been driven onto reservations. Everywhere they turned, there were military people with guns policing their lives. Anyway, when the vision came for the Ghost Dance, it was shared with the many tribes. Red Cloud – an Oglala Sioux warrior – was one of the biggest forces in spreading the Ghost Dance practice. He organized people of many tribes to learn the teachings of Wavoka. Very fast, the Ghost Dance became a shared ceremony."

I nodded as I watched the dancers communing with the dead.

Pipe Carrier went on, "This Ghost Dance caught on faster than any other religion has in this country before or since. The religious leaders of the dance went from reservation to reservation, often risking arrest or even their lives, to spread the dance to many tribes. It was a powerful religion, a belief in the contacting of the dead, and in the protection and even resurrection of the dead. The resurrection of the red world."

I was swaying to the drumbeat.

"But it was also a dance to create freedom from oppression, a kind of war dance against oppression, really protection against further oppression. More like an energy dance. I say energy because war is really about energy. About energy and also about knowledge of energy," Pipe Carrier added. "You see, part of the Ghost Dance doctrine was dedicated to the reclaiming of the land by the red nations, and to the bringing back to life of the sacred buffalo which white man had killed off."

"This doesn't seem to be a war dance," I murmured to myself, still swaying and increasingly mesmerized by the energy.

He must have heard me, because he continued, "The ghost dancers were thought to be dressed for war. But they were really dressed for protection against war, and against the effects of war. It didn't matter to the white man. Anything that might unify the tribes was a threat. Together the red people were potentially quite powerful. Apart they were conquered."

As Pipe Carrier was talking, my body seemed to be tuning into the drums more and more intensely. I couldn't help but move more and more rapidly in rhythm to the quickening beat of the drums, as my whole being was taking in what was being told me by this man. It was as if his words were part of the drumming …. A remarkable sort of wordless message was coming into me.

I was vaguely aware that we had actually become part of the outer field of the Ghost Dance, now that the dance had swelled and engulfed us.

"This physical religion of the Ghost Dance, it was not the real threat to the white world. It was just the understood threat. The true threat was that this ceremony, performed in the most sacred way by the most sacred warrior dancers, protected the souls of the red dead, and guided them safely wherever they needed to go. This dance was known to be able to bring them back when it was time for them to come back."

Pipe Carrier paused, watching the dancers, then went on, "This is, by the way, how whole populations can survive Earthly cataclysms and even genocide. And this is great teaching. And this knowledge, that we have this knowledge, well this is what the white nation sees as a threat – that the red nation knows how to return and will really return in full force. It will survive Earth changes this way. Or at least red medicine women will -- "

Pipe Carrier stopped suddenly and looked at me. "You do understand this, I am sure."

I looked him in the eye and blinked. Did I understand? I said nothing here. Yet, on some level, I was sensing that survival knowledge itself was what was being competed for, fought for. Access to the spirit realm, to be able to come and go to survive in both the physical and the non-physical realms, well this was a key part of this survival knowledge.

The dancers' circles were spinning more rapidly now, in opposite directions. I felt as if a magnetic pull was being generated by this. And my body was being pulled upon by that dual magnetism. The opposing centrifugal and centripetal forces were creating a portal, a key. And a suction it seemed. What did I know about all this? Why was this crossing over into the next world so familiar to me? I was not very surprised at myself now....

"Oh, this is getting good now, can you feel that?" Pipe Carrier waved toward the circle.

"Yes, I feel something strong. I'm feeling pulled in, sucked in."

"Listen carefully right here right now, okay? This is important to you. These people, they are creating a doorway, a sacred opening, a protected space for the dead. This is a sacred window. Only travel through with protection. Can you hear me?"

"Oh ... yeah, sure ... sure." I was mesmerized by the action. Something about the opposing directions of the dancing circles was creating an energetic friction that in turn was creating a suction by way of magnetic void. A vortex. I found my mind lulled into a magnificently gentle floating space, keenly aware of the rhythm of the drums, aware of Pipe Carrier's words, aware of my comments, but aware of much more. There was a sea of something here....

Then, unexpectedly, I saw what must have been a vision, although it looked totally real in the physical world before me. I saw a line of old, old warriors arise right up out of the dust.

Pipe Carrier's voice spoke with vivid clarity right beside me, jolting me a further step. "What do you see?" he asked me in an even voice, "Tell me. What? What?"

Speechless, I raised my hand and pointed toward the fire, to where I could see the warriors still appearing out of the dust right before me.

Pipe Carrier looked there. "Oh yes. You see our ancestors, sister," he said to me simply. "You are blood or you would not be seeing."

With his words, the vision, the drums, the power of the energy opening this portal – I began shaking uncontrollably – my body lost its physical power and I collapsed down to the ground where, a moment before, I'd been standing.

And then I felt the cool rush of angel wings.

9.
pipe carrier

I lost time a while.

Sometime later, Pipe Carrier and I were headed down the mountain again, toward the coast. It seemed to me I had awakened along the way, or maybe once finally back in the truck. How could this be?

We rode a long way without talking, just as we had when heading up to the Ghost Dance. But then Pipe Carrier started talking in his quiet low voice. "Do you want to know what happened, when you collapsed?"

"Well yes, I do."

"Pete, the guy with the rifle, he saw you collapse, and he called the medicine man over. The medicine man, he read you and saw that you had gone over into the land of the dead, like the other dancers who fell to the ground. The medicine man said you had gone to see your red ancestors and to see others in the spirit world."

"He said that?"

"Well, so Pete told me. And he asked me to tell you he is sorry for how he treated you, and that you are invited to come some day and learn more of the Ghost Dance."

I rubbed my eyes, my mind still foggy – and remnants of the dream I had had while I was passed out on the ground flickered through my mind. I must have revealed my surprise about this because Pipe Carrier reacted.

"What is happening? Are you remembering?" he asked.

"I think so. ... I need to watch for a while ... to see it again. I don't know why I can't remember it better."

"Well, you're new at it. We all learn to share our visions when we return from our journeys, but this takes practice. And sometimes the visions are so profound that we're too stunned to pull them out clearly. Then the medicine man makes sense of it for us. I'm no medicine man, but I can listen anyway."

"Well, I found myself somewhere far away, in a place where there had been some kind of destruction, an earthquake maybe," I guessed. I squinted and looked into the night trying to remember the details. "It seemed that there were hundreds of beings, spirits, there – men, women and children. A silence came over everyone gathered there, spirit and flesh alike, and we all, in the same instant, looked up at the sky – or what I thought was the sky – and fell into prayer. We saw a hole in the clouds that were gathered at the horizon – a hole looking something like a doorway. Oh, it was so, so beautiful."

"What did you see? Tell me, please."

"You see, it seemed like there was this vertical rainbow coming out of the doorway and expanding and moving across the land like a moving beam. It made its way down toward us ... the rays of the rainbow ... I counted the rays – Seven of them. Each one was its own colored waterfall of light, washing down from the heavens. The moving light fell upon us like soothing water. Seven colored rays of rushing light washing over us. It was so beautiful."

"Was there more?"

"Well, let me see, ummm – everyone lined up. No one moved. I was confused because I could tell they wanted me to do something. Oh. I felt a pull, a suction, right toward that doorway in the sky. And then I was lifted and carried upward toward that doorway in the sky – by something, I don't know what exactly. I wanted so intensely to go through, I remember. And then ... then ... yes, I can see it now – all the other people – spirits – formed a procession behind me. They were going to follow me through the doorway."

"Then what?"

"Uhm – I can't remember anymore."

"Just close your eyes and relax, and now let yourself see the details of the procession, and the doorway in the sky, and what you felt there."

My eyes closed, a peace came over me, and I was looking at the vision again. I actually started to lead everyone in a certain ritual way, without understanding exactly why or how I was doing so. I told Pipe Carrier, "I started to take them through, there was movement, the feeling was so remarkable – but what's – no – oh no!"

"What is it, what's happening now?"

I saw Fire Star and his warriors, standing there, blocking the doorway and preparing to fight me off, perhaps even to kill my spirit.

"What? Go on, what do you see?" Pipe Carrier insisted.

I couldn't breathe. I was in a panic. "No," I whispered through a throat that was again feeling squeezed shut by massive Fire Star claws. "No more."

"Let me help," Pipe Carrier's voice was saying, "so you won't be left back in the day world to struggle alone with your vision."

"I already struggle with it alone," I muttered. "Every day. Let's drop it now."

"Something stopped this beautiful procession. What was it? Or who?" Pipe Carrier insisted on knowing.

I looked at Pipe Carrier. He was a good person. He was trying to share a vision with me – mine. After all, he had taken me in as his guest. I decided I must honor him with truth. "It'll sound funny to you."

"No it won't. These are the ways we learn about this and about that world and about what's really going on in both places."

"Okay, it was … the Fire Star Tribe leader, Fire Star. He was blocking the doorway in the clouds, he and his warriors. They were there to stop us from going through. Us. Mostly me."

Pipe Carrier's expression dropped. He didn't say a word. He then drove on in complete silence for maybe five minutes. My own heart was cold as ice, there were no thoughts in my mind, there was just blankness – a blankness that kept Fire Star out of my mind.

Then Pipe Carrier spoke abruptly, with vehemence in his voice. "This man, Fire Star, he is not a medicine man. I know he says he is. I know people say he is. But he is not a medicine man. Were you able to stop him, sister?"

I remained numb, barely able to think, let alone talk. The vision was just gone. "I don't know. I don't remember. I can't go to that place. I can't let that man into my mind. Please, don't ask me to do that. Ever."

Pipe Carrier pulled the truck off to the side of the road and turned the engine off. He looked at me closely. "I see this man has done you an injustice."

"It's not everyone's businesses. Just mine, please. So let's keep driving."

"No, the vision, this is all our business. And the injustice hurts all of us. You have to let my warrior friends right this wrong." Pipe Carrier started driving again, but slowly, as if to say he wouldn't push me so hard but meant what he was saying.

"No."

"You must. He stands at the doorway. He blocks our entry."

"I just want to forget what happened, forever."

The whole wave of the rape swept over me again, every moment of it happening as if for the first time … it was horrendous.

"Stop! Stop the truck," I demanded, feeling horribly sick now.

He pulled to the side of the road. I got out fast and vomited at the edge of the highway, until my guts were spasming but empty. Pipe

Carrier held me gently. Then, when the retching was finally finished, he led me back to the pickup and helped me wipe my face.

"Uhhh," I moaned.

Pipe Carrier turned my face to his. His eyes were wide with discovery. "You're the girl I heard about, aren't you? You were having his baby. You're the one, right here with me. You're -- "

"Please!" I raised my voice. "Please, please, please, please. I don't want to talk about this!"

"He forced himself on you, didn't he?"

"Please let's stop this talk."

"But wait, don't you know what --"

"I don't know and I can't know. It's all too painful."

"But don't you know that when a medicine man rapes a woman, all of his power, all of his medicine, is transferred to her?"

I resisted this conversation so very hard that I almost again missed this immense message, one that had been trying to bring on its emergence within me for a while now. And this was far more than just about me. This was about the feminine, the feminine of life and of the Earth, and of our survival, and of the teachings that women were carrying through time, whether women realized this or not.

"No, I don't know and it doesn't make any sense," I said.

"And he can never get it back no matter how hard he tries, even if she is willing to return it to him."

"Please stop. I can't deal with this!" I cried.

Pipe Carrier hung his head. "I'm sorry. Of course I will respect your privacy. But when you are ready, you must accept that this has happened. He raped you and that cannot be erased, and for this I am very sorry. But take the power – it is yours now. He has lost it to you. Whether you want it or not. The medicine will not leave you, whether you want it or not. It will stay with you and surface again and again. Finally, when you are a certain sage age, you will wear the medicine power like a cloak of light. You will see one day that this is true. You have to know this."

I mumbled, still sobbing. "Sure, of course, I know." But I did not really know what he meant. Not yet.

Pipe Carrier started the truck again and we continued driving back to Santa Cruz. I went to sleep. When we got back to Santa Cruz, he dropped me at the house where I was staying. As I was climbing out of the truck, he handed me an address. "I'm going north now. Someone here at this address will always know where I am. If you ever want help with this, just find me. You are my sister. I am your brother. We are blood. This is clear to me. And men of our blood don't do this to women of our blood."

"Well, they shouldn't do it to women of any blood, either."

"I agree. That's true. I agree. Will you be all right? Do you want me to help? I would like to help."

"No. Thanks, really, I'll be okay. Please don't tell anyone you know that that person you heard about could be me. Promise?"

"You have my word. And please think about what I said. About what this means. Promise?"

"Yes, okay, when I'm ready," I answered hollowly.

We said our goodbyes, and lost touch with each other. Some time later, when I was ready and urgently needed to talk about things, Pipe Carrier was not to be located through the address he had left me, and it seemed that no one anywhere had even heard of him.

And so it was that Pipe Carrier had disappeared along with gnome-man and Kiowa – teachers who touched my life, guided me, and left. That seemed to be the way of it. Some stayed, some returned, some moved on. And on.

Maka shan.

10.
loop in sight

I was lost, or something.

For a while, I bounced around, from friend to friend, lost. It seemed that I no longer fit in anywhere. I wasn't who I had once been, whoever I or she had been. And I wasn't who I would eventually be, whoever I or she would be. I was not at all able to redefine or reinvent myself. I searched for some kind of glue, something to put Humpty Dumpty together again. It seemed my persona had no direction.

Eventually, I returned to the place where I had first heard of the Fire Star Tribe. I headed for the house of a professor I knew. He had invited me to come and feel safe for a while. I was relieved and thought time with this wise person would help me.

But this feeling of relief was fleeting. As I climbed the steps to his front door, I was practically accosted by two stern government agents, at least that is what they said they were. They stopped me before I got to the front door, racing around from the side of the house as if they had been there awaiting me.

"There you are, miss."

I was not only startled, I was irritated. "And who are you?"

"We are US Federal Domestic Terror Agents. Please come with us now," they ordered as they showed me their badges.

What choice did I have? There was no way to run, and if there had been, why would I have run? There was no where to go, and no reason either.

I was escorted into a navy blue sedan with government plates on it. After a long, silent ride in the back seat with an armed official, I was feeling sufficiently harassed. My God, what have I done? What on Earth do these people want with me? Why don't I know what it is? I nagged myself.

By the time I found myself in some sort of debriefing room somewhere, my nerves were so frayed that I felt any little thing could press me into hysteria. This is part of their strategy, I warned myself: keep it together. But why? Why? Why was I there?

"Let's get right to the point, miss," the one in charge began.

"Uh, certainly," was all I could think of saying. Sarcasm seemed to be a bad idea at this point, so I held it back.

"Are you acquainted with the Fire Star Tribe?"

"Why do you ask?"

"Are you?"

"Some."

"What does some mean?"

"Somewhat."

"Miss, have you lived with the Fire Star Tribe?"

"Sort of."

"What does 'sort of' mean?"

"For a few months."

"Are you acquainted with its leader?"

"Who?"

"Its leader?"

"I don't really know …."

"Miss --"

"Okay, well maybe."

"What is his name?"

"Name?"

"Name."

"…."

"Miss --"

"Okay, his name is Fire Star, Chief Fire Star they call him, but what is this all about?"

"Fire Star? Does he have any other name?"

"I wouldn't know."

"What is it that Fire Star is doing with these people that he calls his Tribe?"

"I'm not really sure that they are *his* Tribe."

"You're not?"

"Well, no, there seems to be some disagreement about whose Tribe it is, but no one really explained all this to me, so I can't say for sure."

"What is the philosophy of the Tribe?"

"Philosophy?" I wondered what they were really getting at.

"Yes, philosophy. Is there a world view, a belief system, a theory that holds them together – a common purpose?"

"You know, I think you should ask them, not me."

"What would be your best guess about the main world view the Tribe holds?"

"Uh – I guess you could say it is that the world as we know it is coming to an end, and that it is being destroyed by white civilization, and that we should get ready. Something like that."

"Do you believe this, miss?"

"I really don't know what I believe."

"Does this man Fire Star believe this, miss?"

"Why don't you ask him?"

The men looked at each other and then seemed to come to an agreement that one of them would go ahead and explain. "This man Fire Star is missing. Even his own people say they cannot find him. We think he has gone underground."

"Underground? Where? What exactly do you mean by underground?"

"Into hiding."

I shuddered to think of him slinking around stalking me.

"Does this worry you, miss?"

"No, why would it," I asked a little too defensively. One thing was for sure. I wasn't going to tell them I was afraid of Fire Star. If word of this got back to the Tribe, who knows who might come after me. I didn't want any trouble.

"This might worry you because Fire Star is wanted in fifteen states and three countries for an assortment of crimes."

"He is?"

"He is also suspected of organizing takeovers of what his people consider sacred places."

Survivor territories, I told myself as I caught myself muttering "portals." Yes, I said to myself. Probably portals, portals to the spirit world. Maybe they are trying to protect Maka's portals. Or to hoard access to these for themselves.

I must have mumbled something audible, as quite abruptly one of the men said, "Portals?"

"Pardon me?" I asked him.

"Portals, did you say portals? What are those portals?"

"I'm not certain I said portals."

"I believe you did. But do you know what portals are?"

"You mean something like doorways?" Was I playing dumb, or was I actually just ignorant enough to be unable to answer. I could not be certain. Why was I feeling so defensive?

"Young lady, are you aware that there is a massive plan underway to take control of over one hundred specific locations in the US and hundreds more around the world?"

"There is?"

"Yes, and this man Fire Star is the lead orchestrator."

"I really don't think so."

"Why?"

"Because he's so old."

117

These men questioning me looked surprised. "Old?" One of them asked me, "About my age?"

I was embarrassed. This man was maybe in his late forties. "Yes, something around your age, or older."

They laughed a moment and then got serious again.

I fidgeted as I asked, "Am I in some sort of trouble or something? Do I need a lawyer or something like that?"

"No, we don't think you are involved, but your name keeps popping up when we confront Tribe members about Fire Star. They seem to think he is out and about, looking for you."

A horrible sensation raced through my veins – as if shards of glass were in my blood. At that very moment, I knew Fire Star's consciousness had again found me. Not now, NOT NOW! I almost began to cry, and caught myself.

"Are you alright? Would you like water?"

"Yes, please."

"Has this man injured you or held you against your will in any way at any time?"

I was silent. How was I to answer this and how safe was it to answer this? I felt I was in over my head. I drank my water slowly, and then sat there silently looking at the table.

The men decided to talk to each other outside the room. While I waited I heard the sound of drums in my head. My pulse raced to the drum beat as it sped up to a dangerous pace. Boom BOOM. Boom BOOM. Boom BOOM. I wanted to run away. I looked at the only door to the room and saw that these men were blocking the exit. I could not get away.

Now a woman agent came in alone. She handed me water. "Are you feeling alright?" She looked at me with surprising and almost motherly compassion.

"No, I feel sick to my stomach and I want to go home. I am not sure these guys can just keep me here like this, can they? Oh, wait, you're one of them, right?"

"I suppose you can say I am one of them. Don't worry, they're pretty much done. And then I will drive you home."

"Thanks," I whispered and started to cry.

She pulled some Kleenex out of her pocket and studied my face. But she did not ask me any questions. She just waited until I started to talk.

"What is all this about? They are really upsetting me. Why do they think I have any information?"

"Because they have been told that you were the girlfriend of Chief Fire Star, that you were being pulled into place as his co-leader. And that you left him … or ran away from him for some reason. Maybe after ritual rape. Maybe after worse."

Maybe after a great deal of confusion about it all. As much as I tried not to, I started to cry again. I sobbed a few minutes and then got control of myself. I looked at the woman agent. "Look, uh, what's your name?"

"Sally."

"Sally, I am not going to talk about what happened to me there. No one can force me. And about all this underground stuff, whatever, I had no idea what was going on up there and I still don't. I was there for a while and had to leave because I got sick and then I never went back. ... But know this: Not everyone up there is a bad person, in fact most of the people up there are wonderful people who care about the planet very much."

"Yes. Care about the planet." She nodded a yes, seeming to care too.

"They think that the Earth is sacred. Think that the Earth will die if they don't find a way to stop the process." I heard the urgency in my voice and told myself to subdue it.

"Stop the process.... Yes, I think I understand. Pollution is getting out of hand."

"Yes, sort of like that. Even bigger than that," I told her sadly.

"Do you understand that there are many persons wanted by the law living on Fire Star Land? And that much of the Fire Star Land is actually not Fire Star Land?"

"No." What was she trying to tell me. This made no sense.

"Well, just try to stay away from those places, as there is no protection for you there."

"I don't understand."

"I think you do. We cannot protect you there. We also cannot protect you from being associated with any crimes of any one you associate with."

I just stared at her. How could anyone think I was involved with anything? And how could anyone think any crimes were being committed by anyone such as this Fire Star Tribe? They really were not bad people. Most of them had the very best of intentions.

"Take some time to think about it, and call me if you think of more you want to tell me."

"Sure."

She handed me her card. "I'll be right back." She left the room.

I put my head down onto the table, wanting to fall asleep. How could I get this Fire Star to stay out of my mind? And how could I get these people from the FBI or whatever it was to leave me alone. What did Fire Star really want and what did the government really know about him?

The female agent, Sally, returned. "I can take you home now."

"Thank you."

We drove back to the professor's house in silence, just the two of us. And this time I rode in the front seat. When she pulled up in front of the house, she turned off the car as I opened the door to jump out. "Wait a minute, not so fast," she said, but she was not ordering. "Please wait." She put her hand on my arm. "Really. Stay a moment."

"Sure, sorry, thanks for the ride," I told her.

"You're welcome, but that's not why I asked you to wait. There's something you need to know. I know a little more about you than the other guys do."

"About me?"

"Yes, you. I've got several connections to the various Earth Change people. I know that at the Fire Star Tribe, you were considered what they called "the predicted girl," the one who came to take the teachings into the world, to help turn the future away from the predicted disaster. Do you know this?"

I decided to stay a moment longer. I closed the car door and looked at her. How could she know this? I told her, "I don't know what I know. It's all so confusing. The whole thing has put me into a place of intense confusion and desperation. I just want to go on with my life." I didn't add that I would never stop seeking my own key to the sacred realm, that it was my birthright, everyone's birthright ... and that I intended to find it ... and that Fire Star was after me, he thought I took something -- and I had no idea what.

"I don't believe you," this agent, Sally, said.

"Are you accusing me of lying?" Now I studied her face.

"Not really."

"What are you saying?"

"I believe that you discovered things about yourself, things that your visit to the Fire Star Tribe triggered in you. And, that you will never ever forget these things. And you will never ever break your commitment to do the Work."

"The *Work*?" I gasped. How on Earth could she know about the Work? I hardly knew what it was. I just vaguely remembered dreaming my mother had come back to tell me to do the Work. Could she know more than I did about it?

"You heard me. I know about the Work."

"But, you are an FBI agent, or some kind of government employee, not a mystic."

"Sometimes. But I am also a fan of the Seven."

I sat up very straight and my eyes opened very wide. "The Seven?"

"You know what I'm talking about. I know you do."

I was silent. This was getting very strange. Uncannily, eerily, weird.

"Look, Lilith."

I shivered as she called me my birth name, but chose not to contradict her.

"Akashakana, as you are now also called, let me give you some advice."

What? She knew this Akashakana name? "Advice?"

"Don't get caught in the round up. You could be arrested along with any of them that try to implement their take over plan. Don't be mistaken for one of that underground. You are so young and so much not part of the plan. Not that plan anyway. You are part of a larger project. You'll see."

She looked at me to be certain I understood as I shook my head no then yes, more in shock than in denial of what she was saying.

She continued. "I knew I'd see you today. So I bought you something at my own expense, secretly. … Here is a ticket in your name. It will take you to Guatemala City. It's round trip but don't come back for at least three months. And in the envelope with the ticket is one thousand dollars cash. You can live down there on a few dollars a day. So three months plus a little, some one hundred days, works." She put an envelope in my hand and closed my fingers around it.

"What? I can't take this."

"Yes you can. Think of it as an order. Make that money last, it's not much."

I started to cry again.

"Take it and do what I say. Get out of the country for a while. Let this whole thing blow over. Let the plan by the militant wing of the Tribe, the plan to take control, violently if needed, control of the sacred lands in the US, fizzle. Just wait and let these plans fizzle, and then return."

My eyes opened still wider, almost popping out of my head. What was she getting at? Why was she telling me this?

"Look, my great grandmother was a Cherokee too. And Wazine star person. I know the lineage too."

I continued to shake my head in shock.

"Just do what I say. Figure it all out later. Just get out right away. Within five days. Don't tell anyone you are leaving. Visit your father. Don't tell him why you are there, just say you wanted to say hi. Then leave his place in the middle of the night and get to an airport. Leave him a note saying you'll be back in a few months, not to worry, and that you are visiting a friend in New York. Go to Central America right away. Find your way to Uxmal."

"Uxmal? What kind of place is Uxmal? … Excuse me, really, but I have to ask, why should I trust you?"

"Because I know about you and your mother. I actually knew your mother. She taught me about the Work, and once lent me hundreds of dollars. When I tried to pay her back, she told me I would know how to pay her back someday and that I should wait until then. I know all about the Wazine lineage. ... "

I crumpled into a ball, wanting to disappear. The crushing reality of this massive coincidence was too much to bear.

"Sayeth my name if thou wouldst ... " she whispered.

I gazed at her and finished the sentence, the invocation I had learned from my mother: "... travel upon me." And then I started to sob.

"Look, Lilith, I know this is intense, and that you don't want to believe me. But you do believe me. You have no one else to trust right now. Just follow my advice and everything will be okay. You will go on into your long fine life and do the Work you came to do."

"What if I say no?"

"Consider yourself duly warned. Hiding in Central America is a far sight easier than a long long stint in US Federal prison."

"Federal -- ?"

"Yes, violent overthrow, even an attempt at violent overthrow, even a plan for violent overthrow, of the US government is a Federal crime."

"*Violent overthrow?*"

"What do you think we're talking about here, a birthday party? These people are armed and ready to fight."

"I have no idea what you are talking about. Is the United States this close to civil war?" Was this a sign of the Great War to come, I wondered to myself.

"You could say that, but the war we are on the verge of is global."

"Who is right and who is wrong here?"

"It turns out both sides are wrong, because the plan to protect the sacred lands --"

"You mean the portals, don't you?"

"Now you know what the portals are?"

So she had been listening while those men questioned me. "I think they are the sacred openings to --"

"To?"

"Why would I want to tell you?"

"Because I already know. But no need to tell me, just go inside and pack up and get ready to leave."

"I will think about it and call you." I held the envelope in my fist, as tight as I could. This was my ticket to my life, I could feel it. I could feel Sveeka gripping the envelope with all her might right through me.

"No, don't call me. Just do as I suggest. Do not contact me. This would not be a good idea. Go away for a while. Far away. Use the ticket. Find your way to Uxmal, U-X-M-A-L. I mean it."

"I'm not sure why you are helping me, but thank you. Thank you. Thank you."

Yes, Maka Shan," she said earnestly.

"Maka Shan," I echoed, stupefied, oddly vindicated, in absolute awe, as I left the car shaking, "Maka Shan."

I did not tell her I would do as she suggested. Still, I had been waiting for the right time to leave the US. I'm not sure why, but I had been feeling in my gut that I had to. And, Uxmal was indeed calling me, wherever that was. How could this coincidence be anything but a sign that it was time to hear the call? This was it. I would go. And that was that.

Mother Earth take me home. Or somewhere.

Maka. Maka. Maka Shan.

part three:

like rushing water

11.
nothing moves

A yellow fluorescent flickered.

When the somber soldier pushed my shoulder to direct me toward yet another fluorescent-lit office for yet another senseless interrogation, the tarnished silver ring on his leathery hand tangled in my long hair and pulled it hard. In response to the sharp pain, I sucked in a small breath. He glanced around furtively, as if caught in some illicit act, and yanked his hand free, inadvertently or perhaps irreverently tearing out some of my hair. I almost winced but had already decided that the best thing to do in this situation was to remain stoic. They had already detained me against my will for an hour, asking me questions and searching my bags again and again, finding nothing.

I had no idea why I was being held and why my papers were being examined and re-examined by the *aduana*, the customs agents, in the Guatemala airport. There I was, alone, new to the country, spending that one thousand dollars plus my own meager savings on this piece of my quest. I wasn't sure why I had been sent to Guatemala first, but here I was. I was actually thinking about trying to make my way out to the Guatemalan witch doctors or *brujos* as they were called. I had heard quite a bit of talk about them back when I lived with the Tribe. Apparently, most tribes had medicine men (and yes, definitely also medicine women -- although in many cases these women were quiet about their real work, as I was going to discover.)

I couldn't have known that the customs agents suspected I was one of a group of European terrorists – who had purportedly fled to Central America. Finally, apparently, or at least temporarily, the Guatemalan officials let me go. They ascertained that I was just some young and, at least for the time being, harmless, American woman foolish enough to travel by herself into Central American territories which were at the time pocked by sporadic outbreaks of violent and, seemingly to outsiders, indiscriminate *guerilla* warfare. One of the officials actually apologized to me after my detainment and then revealed to me the details of this case of mistaken identity. I smiled as innocently as I could and told him that "*claro pues, yo no soy una terrorista*" – that of course I was not a terrorist. I was so glad to be released – free – that I did not complain about the unnecessary and disrespectful detainment and treatment I had received upon my arrival in this country.

As soon as I was released, I headed out of the airport into the ancient land whose modern name is Guatemala. I was surprised at how loud the capital city, Guatemala City, sounded. It confused me to land amidst such an entanglement of humanity. I had allowed myself to fantasize that I was coming to a mecca of pristine beauty, indigenous mysticism, and protected native life. But clearly, this was a land in transition, a place struggling to balance the crescendo of its sloppy modernization with the precious symphony of its ancient Mayan and other Native heritage. I reeled, grabbed the first taxi I could, and asked to be driven to the bus station where I would buy a ticket.

I was headed for the mountain villages I had heard about, the area where I was certain I would learn more about the ancient indigenous cultures and their ancient indigenous access to the spirit realm. Maybe they could teach me what I wanted to learn – to travel to my star home. I was certain that this skill was embedded in most ancient teachings and that some tribe somewhere would share what remained of this technique with me. Why not the descendants of the great Mayans? And maybe, just maybe, they would know the Seven and how to call them. After all, Kiowa had recognized the vision of the Seven as a sign. There must be more information about this kind of contact to be had, I told myself.

So I was headed into what I assumed would be great revelation and absolute truth, late at night, amidst wall-to-wall people, in a ramshackle bus which seemed certainly bound to lose its doors and tires with each new bump. Everyone was staring at me. They looked like a mouthful of faces, wanting to swallow me with their eyes. Of course I stuck out like a sore thumb. But I kept telling myself I had as much right to be there as anyone else did. After all, I was born on this planet too – at least my body was.

I looked back at the sea of people's eyes. They all looked so serious, and so placid. I wondered if their children ever cried. I wondered why so many eyes were upon me. I guessed that it was because I was the only American, the only relatively light-skinned person, the only tall person, and a young woman alone. Even though I had what felt like not enough money on me and wondered how I would make it through this three month plus long trip, I figured that they were looking at me as if I were wealthy.

Five hours later, when I finally stepped off the bus into this disturbing chapter of my search, I discovered what at least some of these people believed themselves to be staring at. A serious little boy came up to me through the dust cloud we were all enmeshed in and touched my arm. For some reason, instead of asking for money as I thought he would do, he just gazed at me in awe. I knelt down and offered him some candy that I had been saving for someone just like him. But instead of accepting it, he touched my hand, looked at me, and said breathlessly, "*Una extraterrestria.*"

An extraterrestrail? What on Earth could he mean? "*Extraterrestria?*" I said, still kneeling.

The boy's face broke into a gentle smile. "*Claro pues, si, tu – una extraterrestria, no sabes?*" he asked me: of course, yes, you are an extraterrestrial, don't you know?

Next I knew, there were several children around me saying the same thing.

I stood up and looked around. It seemed the entire busload of people had encircled me. A very short, old woman, wrapped in a red woven shawl and wearing black, waddled up to me. I looked at her with questioning eyes. She murmured at me, *"Hay otras extraterrestrias aqui ... en las montanas...."* and pointed at the mountains on the horizon. What did she mean, there are other extraterrestrials here, in the mountains?

I tried to get more information. *"Que son extraterrestrias?"* What are extraterrestrials? I asked her, wanting to know what her people thought these beings were.

She looked at me almost comically as if to say she understood my joke and was not going to be fooled by my feigned innocence. She pointed at me, calling out loudly, *"Extraterrestria! Mujere extraterrestria!"* Extraterrestrial woman!

The small crowd rushed at me and began petting and touching me. All right, I told myself, they think – or maybe they KNOW – that I am an extraterrestrial – that I come from the stars. How can this be? How can these people automatically see what I have looked so hard and long to find a way to express back home? How can they understand one of the most critical issues in my life better than I do?

I asked them how to find the other extraterrestrials and they directed me to a place in the mountains. I determined to make my way there. After all, the information had found me. The indication was that I was on, at least generally speaking, the right track, (for at least this). Of course, this wasn't in the direction of Uxmal where I had been sent. Still, I had time for this seeming side journey. And I felt very drawn in this side journey direction. Anyway, I had to spend quite a bit of time floating around Central America, so why not, I said to myself.

Maybe now I would discover the best way home to the land of the Seven, my ancient ancestors.

Following directions, I walked out toward what was, in those days of the 1970s, before modern tourism smothered it and changed its face forever, the edge of a lovely old village. This little stroll became for me more of an excursion through a museum of Central American life than a walk from one place to another. Set against a background of piercing beauty and color, saturated with brilliant flowers and profound volcanic forms waiting out the eons of centuries, there were the insulting Pepsi and Coca Cola signs. The land of paper people and dead ground was already, back in those years, invading this sacred terrain.

I stopped and bought for a few cents several bottles of water, two bottles of juice, chewing gum, and a bag of nuts, assuming incorrectly that I would find a place to eat later, when I needed to eat a meal. At the end of the road, I found a beautiful lake resting innocuously like a sleeping animal in what seemed to be an old volcano. In the distance I saw a military policeman – an MP, or *soldado* as these men were called – carrying a long gun, a rifle, and looking for someone who might be hiding under a disintegrating boat dock. Men with him, not in uniform, carrying machete-like knives, seemed to be assisting in the search. Probably looking for those terrorists, I said to myself – one of which I am not so I needn't worry – I reminded myself.

The far side of the lake appeared sparsely populated, if that. Not wanting to waste even an hour let alone a day, I found a young fisherman who would, for an American dollar, take me by boat across the lake. I was enthusiastic and we took off presently although he seemed a little hesitant to do so. I was already in the middle of the lake when I thought, prompted by my sudden realization that we were taking on water, to scrutinize the little boat for its safety.

I decided that I was as likely to make it across the lake on top of the water in this boat as I was to have to swim the rest of the way. It was a huge lake. Would I make it across if I had to, I asked myself calmly. I found the water inviting. But when I reached down to touch it, I found it was brutally cold and foreboding rather than inviting. And, the moment I touched the water, as if by magic, both the air and the lake became stormy. Clouds came from out of nowhere and the sky transformed to ominous. I didn't like how I felt now. Surprised. Queasy. But instead of fear, I just felt a nagging doubt that I'd make it across.

For a brief moment, way out there on the lake, my mind yanked into my preoccupied consciousness that old memory of my mother reading to me from the *Egyptian Book of the Dead*, which she had done on many occasions when I was between the years of six and twelve or so. Yes, pretty young for such stuff, but it fascinated me. As child, I had been mystified and overawed by large bodies of water. "*Sayeth my name,*" my mother had read to me, "*Sayeth my name if thou wouldst travel upon me.*" I could actually hear her voice now, "*Sayeth my name if thou wouldst travel upon me.*"

Sayeth my name. I heard this phrase several times, it resonated all around me, as if it were coming from the water below me.

"Okay fine, I'll say your name," I mumbled. What did I have to lose? "Lago, lago, lago, lago, lago, lagahhh, lagah. – lagatla, agatla, atla, atla, atlannnn, atlan." I stopped, unaware that my chanting had altered the syllables into new forms and sounds. I hadn't noticed that I had moved into saying *"atlan"* which is a word showing up in numerous indigenous languages of the Americas and other regions of the Earth, standing for a land that had long disappeared – much like the continent described in ancient Mediterranean stories of Atlantis.

It would be years before I would realize what I had come to be chanting during that rough and mystifying crossing. It would be years before I would understand that Atlan was actually a place in the past, the essence of which – and perhaps even the material reality of which – could be summoned into the present by invoking its name while in a precisely defined state of mind.

It was this very state of mind that ancient medicine women saw future people would need to navigate themselves through the coming dramatic shifts in the Earth's material plane – and beyond. Long ago, the invocation of Atlan had been taught by the ancient priestesses to those who were to pass it on in such a way that it would be preserved for modernity. This Atlan invocation was to be released in its entirety in the future when the time of Earth change, the *Maka Shan*, had come again. But then these sacred Maka Shan teachings of these priestesses were repressed, shut down, hidden away. So, to protect these essential teachings through time, great sacrifices were made … and well ….

I would eventually come to know that I, along with many others, had been called on my journeys by these ancient priestesses. Fantasy, mythology, might have carried and protected these teachings through time, but reality would call us to know them now.

Well, anyway, the little boat rocked more and more roughly and even my young captain now looked quite concerned. I saw him cross himself hastily several times and mumble as he looked at the changed sky with surprise. Now I became strangely aware of the lake herself, as if she were a presence. I thought to myself that maybe it was my exhaustion that was causing me to squint at the water's surface now, to see something there, as if it were a face. The boat rolled from side to side, hardly moving forward at all. The swelling lake seemed to be alive. This body of water had seemed to me to be an animal, her silvery coating rising and falling as if she were breathing.

I suppose I could die here, I said to myself. But I won't, I told myself resolutely.

"No you won't," I heard Seven voices say in unison.

I closed my eyes and called Kiowa. Kiowa. Kiowa. Kiowa. I waited for some kind of answer. I didn't know whether to attribute it to wishful thinking or to the spirits, but I heard an answer. It was Kiowa's voice. *"Like rushing water. ... like rushing water. ... just become the water. Just be like rushing water."* A disturbing urgency filled me. I was in danger out there. Even Kiowa, where ever he was, knew.

"Sayeth my name," I heard a voice say.

I was startled. "Sveeka?" I whispered. A quick picture of my mother sitting at the edge of a river and telling me something formed in my eyes. What was she saying?

A quick verbalization formed in my ears: "You are in the lineage. It is tradition that I would pass these teachings on to you, my first born daughter."

It was Sveeka!

"Sveeka!" I shrieked aloud as the boat almost capsized.

"Sayeth my name!" I heard her command.

Having no other immediate options, I did. "Altan. Atlan. Atlan." I closed my eyes and imagined that I was part of the tumultuous swelling and moving water beneath me. "*Like rushing water nothing moves. Like rushing water nothing moves,*" I repeated under my breath. I could feel the panicky eyes of the now very concerned boatman upon me, yet I kept my lids shut and stayed with the concentration I was generating.

Sure enough, sometime into this process – I don't know how long – I relaxed. And so did the lake. The water changed. Just like that.

· · · · · · ·

I don't know how much time passed, but when I opened my eyes, the sky was clear, the lake calm, and the once distant beach right before us. My young boat man delivered me quite unceremoniously and sopping wet onto that small beach dotted with a few old *pangas* – fishing boats – most of which looked as if they would leak, fill and sink. I decided to think about getting back across, to the place from which I had started, later. I had places to go and people to see, I told myself, wherever and whomever they may be.

Maka called me.

Shan.

Maka shan.

12.
mountain bruja

There I was.

At one end of the beach, there was a small stream winding out into the lake. There were some women -- Seven of them – all wearing their hair in long black braids, covered in deep reddish maroon colored clothing, washing clothes on rocks. I told myself that maybe they could tell me how to find the brujo that lived on this mountain. I approached the women. They didn't look up even though my footsteps announced themselves by grinding on the stoney beach. I stopped about five feet away from the oldest woman and cleared my throat. Still no attention was paid me.

For some reason beyond the obvious explanation, which was that I was intruding and was not being received with great aplomb, I felt shy. I watched them pound the wet fabric of their laundry with stones, rock hitting rock, the clothes laid out on larger rocks as they received this treatment. Finally I managed to summon my reluctant voice. *"Por favor,"* I asked, please, *"direcciones para a var a el brujo que vive en este Montana,"* directions to go to the medicine man who lives on this mountain.

The old woman did not look up or make any gesture at all in the form of an answer. Did she want money, I stupidly wondered. I pulled some of my limited change out of my pocket and reached toward her with it in my open palm. She didn't look at me but she looked at the money and shook her head no. I knelt, squatting close to the ground, hoping to make eye contact. And this I did. At least I think I can call this eye contact.

She turned her head slowly to see me. When she looked up at me, she somehow bore her vision right into my head, drilling me with her deep black eyes. I felt needles of a strange, bewildering energy pricking my skin. I felt a powerful jolt of something race through my body. For a moment, I thought my bones would crack and burst, and then I found myself falling backward what seemed an eternally long way. I landed on my rear end, gasping. Trying to recompose myself, I held my eyes glued to the Earth.

"*Mada durahzha*," the old woman whispered. Then she mumbled something more, barely audible, in a language that was clearly not Spanish. "*Steend gwah, steend gwah zageah. Ooyrreet-yeeahhh.*" It almost made sense to me, as if I remembered the meaning of her words.

A mix of confusion and surprise bloomed in my chest. What were these words? How could I know something of these words? What did I know? Where had I heard them before? How could I even vaguely recognize their sound, their rhythm?

Humbled by her surprising power, I gathered myself enough to look back at this old woman. I had to look upward just a little. She was standing now. I realized that she was very very, very short, shorter than the gnome-man I had met in the freight train. The gnome-man? Oh yes, the gnome-man, I told myself. I thought of him for a moment.

The old woman reached out and handed me a dirty bundle of red yarn wrapped around two small pieces of wood. At first the bundle looked like some dirty scraps found on the ground somewhere. My fingers tried to make sense out of the entanglement. The old woman reached down and moved the sticks around until they crossed each other. As she did, I felt her hands. They were so tough that they felt like the soles of eternally shoeless feet. Her rearrangement of the sticks pulled the yarn into a diamond-shaped weaving.

"*Dazah*," the woman commented pointing at the diamond.

"*Que*?" What? I asked her. "*Lo ciento, no intiendo.*" I'm sorry, I don't understand.

"*Ojo de dios*," she murmured, switching to Spanish, and still pointing at the yarn diamond. "*Para su proteccion.*"

The eye of God for my protection? As I was wondering what relevance this had to my request for directions to the *brujo*, the old woman made a clicking sound with her tongue.

A large red bird appeared, out of the blue, on a nearby rock. How could I have missed it flying in? "*Su viaje ... un volar. Verda?*"

Your journey, a flight, true? What kind of question was this? I shrugged and stood up, awkward about the fact that I was hovering over her short body. She pointed at the dirt road and then up at a small dip in the horizon of the mountain.

I nodded. This was where I was to go.

In those early years of my lifelong pilgrimage, even after all I had been through, I was able to walk off into the mountain jungle so trustingly, so naively, on faith. So I followed her directive. I nodded in appreciation and attempted to pay the woman. She would take no money. She also would not let me hand her back the *ojo de dios*. Instead she pressed it into my hand and pressed my hand over my heart. Then she pointed at the sky. "*Su familia*," she said in Spanish. My family. "Familia del las estrellas Sietes," she added. Family from the Seven stars? Really? Here too?

Your family, she had said to me. I truly marveled at the realization that she knew this. Why? How? It was clear enough to me that all of this was either a riveting coincidence or no coincidence at all. I decided to live with the riddle. I bowed a little, in gratitude, and turned to leave.

The woman waited until I was about ten feet on my way and shouted toward my back in a deep wind-filled voice, "*Deehcha, deehcha, gwa dazah!*" in that other language again.

I felt a strong wind come up out of the otherworldly calm that had embalmed us there. I stopped in my tracks and did not turn around to see what she was doing.

I was, for a moment, very cold, chilled by something that came from deep in the Earth and not from the sudden wind.

"*Mire!*" she called out. Look!

I spun around to see whatever it was she was asking me to see. She was pointing at the sky. I looked up. I definitely couldn't believe

146

my eyes. There was that same kind of small cloud in that same kind of otherwise clear sky, striped by those same brilliantly glowing Seven colors. These were the Seven colors of the rainbow, yes, brilliantly glowing colors, colors that I had seen summoned during a Fire Star Tribe ceremony, colors I had also seen the gnome-man show me as we left the freight train in Saint Louis.

"*Siete rayes, para usted.*" Seven rays, for you, she said.

I dropped my bag and just watched the rainbow for several minutes. Yes, I had indeed seen this during ceremony when I lived with the Fire Star Tribe. And yes, I had definitely seen it again when the gnome-man pointed it out after we left the freight train. And now here it was. Now, when the old woman on the beach clapped her hands, it faded abruptly. How had she known I needed to see this reminder of the path that had led me here – this marker on my path? Had she somehow summoned this sign that was so shockingly familiar to me – summoned it with her invocation? Yes, it seemed to be so.

Now I gazed at this woman from a distance. In the wind, a dust spiral formed and whirled toward her. She made no effort to dodge this flying dirt and instead, when it encompassed her, she raised her arms to the sky. For a moment, she looked like a bird, her arms appearing to be large wings about to fly her away.

Oh gosh, she's the bruj*a*, there is no bruj*o*, no medicine *man*, she's the medicine *woman* I'm looking for, I told myself. Now what? Can I make some real contact with her? How?

The wind stopped. She looked as if she had heard me and seemed accepting of my discovery. I took a step toward her. She shook her head no and pointed me up the mountain again, as if to insist I be on my way.

I did what she directed and headed off the beach to the mouth of what now seemed to me to be a practically alive dirt road. *Mother Earth, take me, send me home. Moo-tah-hoh Tehrr-ha, vozhlahz wo meestirhey-yah.* Maka maka maka shan, I'm looking for your truths.

…

When I looked back, the old *bruja* had gone back to washing clothes on the rocks. Now she was alone it seemed. She did not look my way, but several – Seven it seemed -- whirlwinds of dust spiraled around her. I shook my head in disbelief, but the whirlwinds continued whirling. Certain that this was not a natural development, I assumed the old *bruja* had generated them. "Just another everyday miracle," I murmured.

I went to head up the road. Just before the beach was entirely out of my sight, I needed just one more glance back and, of course, I took it. Maybe this was a mistake, I don't know. But when my eyes looked back, they saw the old *bruja* standing there talking to Sveeka, who was coming into focus out of one of the whirlwinds.

For some reason, this sight spooked me. I immediately turned away to run up the road. "Oh no, this can't be," I scolded myself.

While running off, I took one more quick look back and saw nothing and no one there but the women who had been washing their laundry on that beach when I had arrived.

"You see," I teased myself, "it was just your imagination …
yeah, right," I told myself and marched on without reservation. The
truth was calling, wasn't it?

It was good that I had, much earlier, on the other side of the
lake, bought something to drink and some nuts, because there were no
opportunities for eating or drinking along the way. I walked alone for
an hour before I began to question myself as to my direction and
purpose. I had come a long, long way … for … for … *for what
exactly*? I sat down on the side of the road and rubbed my eyes. I was
about to take a drink when a *soldado*, soldier, with a rifle appeared. A
gun. Not again.

I nodded at him pleasantly.

"*Passeporte*?" Passport, he demanded and held out his hand
while still holding the gun with the other.

I suppose I could get shot here, I told myself. "*Si, senor.*" Yes
sir. I dug out the hidden pocket bag hanging from my neck under my
shirt, containing my passport and other identification. I handed it all to
him.

He studied the contents of my pocket bag. He seemed satisfied
with my papers, however, apparently, my satisfactory papers were not
enough – there was another problem of some sort. Now he waved his
rifle and indicated that I was to walk ahead of him on a path into the
jungle. I didn't like this situation. I just wanted to get up the mountain
to see the *brujo*. BrujA. What kind of price was I paying for just a bit
of knowledge?

Ahead of me, I saw an elaborate series of *palapa*-type structures peeking out from the dense jungle forestation. A sun burned beer-bellied American man in a Hawaiian shirt and swim trunks, carrying a beer and a newspaper, emerged. "Oh, what did you find, Jaime?" He waved me in through a doorway that smelled of tortillas and fried meat. He waved the soldier away.

"Sit," he ordered.

I sat. So did he, facing me. "What brings you here?" he queried suspiciously.

I somehow knew that my *brujo*-brujA story wouldn't be a good one in this context. "Well, I am a painter and a photographer and I think this is a beautiful place. I wanted to explore this mountain and make some sketches and take some shots."

He looked as if he didn't believe me. "You alone?"

I figured that I'd better not seem to be alone in my wanderings here, even though I was. Everyone knew a woman shouldn't travel alone. Everyone but me. "Well, no, not really. My friends are also artists and they are hiking around here too," I explained.

It seemed that he still didn't believe me. "Where are they right now?"

"I don't know. Probably down by the shore. They'll be looking for me soon though."

The American raised his eyebrows and nodded leeringly. I could see that he realized I was trying to protect myself from him. "Look, young lady, we've had terrorists. They say they're freedom fighters – and other trouble causers -- bombing and exploding things, and threatening to kidnap and kill around here. And we just don't want any more."

"Oh, I see, well, I'm not here to cause any trouble. Why would anyone come all the way out here to cause any trouble?"

He narrowed his eyes at me after I asked this question, but then he relaxed. "This is a plantation owned by a multinational corporation, which many say should get out of Guatemala and out of all native jungles. Some kind of stuff about sacred lands or something like that."

"Oh."

He stood up and went to the stove against the wall. "Tortilla and beans?"

"No thanks." I should have said yes. I was going to find myself hungry later. "I would, however, like to go now."

"You would, would you?"

"Well, yes, that is my right."

"I don't think you understand, young lady. You aren't in the USA here. This is not a democracy, this is a police state. And you are on private property – on the property of a private plantation operated under contract with this country's police state government. You are trespassing, my dear, and more. You are committing several crimes for which you can be arrested and held indefinitely in this political climate."

"Oh." I wondered what to do with this information. Maybe I could apologize. "I'm very sorry, and I had no idea that I was trespassing. I would like you not to report me to the police. I haven't done anything wrong and I mean no one harm."

He looked at me and softened. "I have a daughter about your age. She's married and lives in Ohio. That's where you should be. Home. What're you doing way out here in this God-forsaken place?"

It didn't seem to me that God had forsaken it. White paper people had, or were beginning to. "As I said, looking for things to paint and photograph."

"Tell you what, you can go on up the road a ways. It's private property, but I give you official permission. The road ends soon and then you'll have to turn around, though."

"Thank you."

I stood up to leave.

"And if you need a place to stay on the way down, I have one."

I shook my head no.

"It's a guest room. My kids stay there when they visit. You'll be all right there. The door locks, if that's what you're wondering."

"Well actually I was, but thank you. I'll see how far I get."

"Jaime, show this woman out and let her be."

Jaime appeared from just outside the door now speaking English. "Sure, Mr. Matsen."

That was it. I was escorted back to the road and headed on alone.

13.
flaming rainbow

I walked for about thirty minutes.

Then I found a side road that seemed to head uphill more rapidly than the one I was on. I walked up this steeper road another half-hour or so and came to a cluster of shabby shacks. A woman was seated in the doorway of one of them. I decided to ask her about the *brujo* or *bruja* I was seeking. Maybe she would send me back to the old woman by the lake, and Sveeka, and then I would know … but know what exactly? Know what? What was I looking for?

That ongoing undercurrent of confusion continued to stream through me. I was growing used to it, at least somewhat. I was adapting more and more to my not knowing the why, what and where regarding my journey….

Now I walked over to the woman in the doorway and pointed to the top of the mountain, asking "brujo?" She looked at me with wide eyes and waved me into the shack. I followed her in. She motioned for me to sit down near an old woman who was weaving on a make shift loom crafted out of string and branches. All the young woman said was, "K'nah'koo'd-ah," as she nodded to the old woman." I assumed this was the old woman's name.

I nodded at the old woman as well and said her name as well, "K'nah'koo'd-ah." She acknowledged me with a brief nod and then resumed her weaving. My eyes ached with an eerie sense of surprise. Hadn't I just seen her by the lake? Wow, she was here already? Actually, I wasn't very surprised now, which surprised me most.

I looked around me. There were twenty-some candles burning, the flames' reflections leaping off of the skulls of dead animals that hung from the walls and the ceiling. Long braids and ponytails of hair without people's heads and bodies to go with them hung from the walls between the skulls. There were teeth and beads and bones of all kinds all over the place – in bowls and jars and loose on table tops and shelves and on the floor. Leaves and branches of various trees and plants hung upside down from the ceilings, presumably to dry. Flower petals lined the makeshift windowsills, including the one through which sun light poured over the loom where the old woman was weaving.

"*Ola*," I said in my broken Spanish. Hello. The old woman didn't answer. I waited a moment. I decided that introductions were neither being asked for nor wanted here. I looked at what she was weaving. It was precisely detailed and exquisitely crafted. "*Que es esto? Es muy muy bonita.*" My compliment did not do it justice.

"*Jaspe*," she answered in a whisper without stopping her work.

"*Que?*" I hadn't quite understood her. What?

She sounded out the word for me, "*Hos-pay.*"

"*Jaspe*," I responded.

"*Si, jaspe.*"

The younger woman fed the fire on the other side of the room. Then she began to stir a pot. As she did, she chanted something in a language that sounded like the language of the *bruja* on the beach. I began asking the older woman how she made the beautiful jaspe and she began explaining, mostly in gestured sign language. This plus later research explained the art of jaspe to me. Basically, there were two looms. Both were strung with their respective colors of threads, usually in rows of colors. The one or both, depending on the degree of complexity desired in the final weaving, were painted with a regular series of sacred patterns. The final step was to pull, one by one, each thread off of one of the looms and weave it onto the other, preserving the arrangement of the threads and designs being pulled from the first loom. The end result was a gorgeous and visually complex tapestry of two intersecting designs, two visual mantras meshed.

K'nah'koo'd-ah stopped and looked me in the eye, as she gestured at her weavings. "*Una historia de vida, y de Terra.*" A history of life, and of Earth. The complexity and beauty of the weaving called *jaspe* captured for this woman all there was about this world and its interwoven streams and patterns. But it seemed to be more – a tapestry with not only a story but a will – a will to carry information within it.

Her work stopped and she went to sit by the fire, beckoning me to follow. This I did. She and the young woman, plus a few other women who had come in, engaged me in a ceremony, in what I

155

figured was their native or maybe special sacred language. This ceremony involved the passing of a skull and the throwing of something which smelled sweet – later I learned it was rose water – over themselves and me. The old woman got up and began waving her hands around me, much the way the gnome-man had done. I experienced an instant remembrance of the waves of energy racing through my body that he had triggered by his gestures. What was this coincidence? Were they of the same tribe? How had I found these wonderful women who knew this wonderful magic?

The room had become dark unnaturally fast. The sky was breaking open with thunder and rain. A bolt of lightning hit the sill of the makeshift window. The hairs on my arms stood on end. Another bolt struck in the same place. The lightning had almost come into the room and hit us: I could feel its static traces throughout my flesh. The women were chanting loudly now. The thunder was booming almost continuously. The old woman got up, continued her chanting, and leaned out the window. Now she looked up and shouted at the sky. She ceased her chanting and stepped back a few feet. Another bolt of lightning hit in the same place. She stomped her feet. Now another bolt! Another stomp. Another bolt! She closed her eyes, clapped her hands three times and the storm stopped. She beckoned me outside and pointed to the sky.

By now, I shouldn't have been surprised to see what I saw, yet I was. The sky had cleared overhead, except for a small cloud that yes, wore a bright strip of rainbow on it.

"*Siete rayes,*" Seven rays, the old woman said.

"*Si, siete rayes,*" I whispered wide-eyed. I shivered. So it's the Seven rays again, the sign marking the path, the mysterious sign, I said to myself. At least I know I'm onto something. … But what? What? What? Oh, for all these Goddesses' sakes, what?

"*Si, las siete rayes del ama de el ojo de dios. El portal.*" Yes, the Seven rays from soul of the eye of god. The portal. Now she speaks of the portal, just the way the gnome-man did, I said to myself in awe. I felt like a detective unraveling a great mystery.

"*Donde es el brujo de este montana?*" I finally had the guts to ask where the medicine man of the mountain was.

Both women began to laugh. "*BrujO? BrujO? BrujO?*" they kept asking me, emphasizing the 'O' at the end of the word. I should have known better.

"BrujA," I said, correcting myself.

Finally, the younger woman spoke up and explained that, "Si. *No hay brujOs nunca aqui, hay solomente brujAs.*" I took this to mean that there were no medicine MEN here on this mountain, only medicine WOMEN.

"*Ellas tienen las secretas del tiempo. Son las guardinas angeles de las verdas ancianas de las Olmecas, Mayans, Lacandones, Quiches y otras tribas orginales de este mundo.*"

I mulled this over. Okay, I was being told that: These women have the secrets from time. They are the guardian angels of the ancient truths of the Olmecs, Mayans, Lacandones, Quiches, and other original tribes that lived in every part of this world.

I sat down. I realized that I had been finding the objective of my search all along the way. The three old women, the one at the bus station, the one on the beach, and now this one, were keepers of magic and knowledge. I had been seeking *them*, not a medicine *man*. And I had sort of known this all along. Why hadn't I seen who they were and how they had appeared to me? Was I myself so gender-biased as to have missed the fact that they were women? I promised myself that I would never make that mistake again.

I peered curiously at these humble women in their earthy environment. However, I felt now, on every level of my self and soul, that this was a protected enclave, one of the last bastions, one of the secret hiding places for ancient teachings. But these women were emphasizing the females in their tradition – insisting that it was the females who had preserved the true teachings. What was this – a sort of age-old feminism? But it wasn't. It was maybe even most essential truth.

As if my thoughts had been heard, via an imperious gesture, the older woman urged the younger to communicate more to me. The younger one nodded and obeyed, reverently lighting Seven candles before beginning and then chanting something unintelligible to me as she knelt before them. Then the women prayed together – I assumed it was prayer – they extended their arms, palms upward, to the sky and looked directly upward. Next they moved their hands and arms in synchrony through a series of gestures, pausing a moment to hold each of the several poses and chant a further piece.

When they had completed, the younger woman – who by now I realized was her teacher's, K'nah'koo'd-ah's, apprentice – lit a branch and let it smolder a moment before moving toward me and waving it around me. This action was similar to the smudging tradition I had seen when I lived with the Fire Star Tribe, beginning just before my first sweat lodge. Here I could tell I was being purified for ceremony, and sensed it was before an induction into a level of truth or teaching they wanted me to attain. What? Why me? Why? Why me? Why here? No answers yet.

But it was clear to me – and I am not sure how this was clear but this was clear -- these women were the remnants of some priestess sect, a very ancient one. Knowing this came over me, into me, somehow.

I was in no way ready for what happened next. They all clapped their hands in unison and the fire in the makeshift hearth roared up to a wild state. I was worried it would spread but they apparently were not worried. The younger woman took a tiny knife and held it over the flame. After a few minutes of this, she removed it and seemed to hold it in the air to cool. The she handed it to K'nah'koo'd-ah, who beckoned me closer.

What on Earth was this they were asking me to participate in? An initiation ceremony? Any compunctions to resist were overridden by my intense curiosity and drive for information regarding whatever I sensed was this ancient sacred of the feminine. Back then, I had very little idea what this ancient sacred of the feminine was, but I felt its reality on a gut level. I sat on my knees on the ground before old

K'nah'koo'd-ah. She reached over and pointed to my little finger on my left hand. The younger woman grabbed it and sprinkled some fluid – it smelled like rose water – on it. Then old K'nah'koo'd-ah took my hand, laid it on her knee, and quickly, before I could stop her, made a small but deep incision on my finger. I stared at my finger a moment, wincing. It was a while before it bled. When she saw my blood, the old woman squeezed my finger and held it over a small rock until a few drops of blood fell onto it. The younger woman then took the rock from her, holding it as if it were precious and standing before the fire. They both murmured a song, or chant. Then they paused and looked at me as if I knew what this was all about.

"*Mire, mire, mire...*" Look, look, look, they directed me, pointing at the fire. The younger woman tossed the rock carrying my blood into the flame.

I stared in awe at the result. A single flame emerged, far taller than the rest of the fire, its glow surging in undulating waves of successive colors, glowing from the yellow gold of the fire's flame, to an amber orange, to a crimson magenta, to a billowy pink, to a dark mysterious purple, to an royal indigo blue, to a lighter sky blue, to a glowing chartreuse green the color of new leaves shining in the sunlight – then back to indigo -- after which the single flame extinguished itself and the previous fire remained.

I looked at the women for an explanation, however they were also in awe and too busy rejoicing, celebrating this apparently astounding and wonderful event, to explain anything to me. They leapt up, danced, and sang, and began to adorn me with necklaces, flower petals, and leaves, touching my head over and over.

Eventually, they settled down and sat facing me, saying nothing, looking at me expectantly again – for a long time.

What did they want?

Their silence seemed to extend to an eternity. Yet, the eternity was a comfortable one. It was within the fold of this timelessness that I got it – somehow I got it. I had not only been initiated, I had been discovered. I don't know how I realized this. The communication was not one with which I was familiar. I realized then, as I still realize now: how easy it is to miss out on important information coming to us by not seeing its unusual form of delivery as a form of anything at all. I also realized then, as I still realize now, that the discovery that had just then taken place was far bigger than we were. And I wasn't the only one having this sort of experience. My experience was virtually universal, one of many. This was a part of the discovery the human race was making about its knowledge, its history and its future.

I peered at these women in wonderment. A magical light, barely visible to the eye, filled the space around us, like chalk dust. In this space and state of mind, with these women gazing at me knowingly, I experienced a pure and complete and instantaneous collapse of all my preconceptions. I was no longer in a hut in mountainous Central American country – a region faced with the invasion of the paper people and the coming of the dead ground. I was transported to another place and another time, one entirely foreign to me and yet entirely familiar. It was as if we women had been sitting together for eons, waiting for the turn of time – this very turn of time – to come. And now here we were, just as we had always been – crones sitting on the edge of time, holders of some form of wisdom. And we were reflecting many others elsewhere, who were doing the same, and are doing, will be doing, before then, then, now, and in the time to come – the same.

This much I knew. But what was I to do with this etheric awareness?

The older woman nodded a slight bow at me. "Esquipulas."

What did this mean?

"*Tu sabes Esquipulas?*" Did I know Esquipulas, she wanted to know.

"No."

"*Es-ki-poo-laaaas. En tres semanas, tu vas al Esquipulas.*" In three weeks, I should go to Espquipluas, she said to me. "*Muy importante.*" Very important.

So it was a place, a destination. I cannot explain why I agreed to go. "*Si, como no,*" yes, why not? I agreed to make a journey to I did not know what. But wasn't that like the rest of my trip here on this planet?

I had come to the mountain and found what I now understood was what I needed to find: the next directive – the next step in my pilgrimage. It is funny how, if you are paying attention, you are guided through life – your pilgrimage, no matter how painful or confusing, is mapped at each step of the way. There is nothing ambiguous about the process if you know it is going on.

I walked back down to the lake, with a keen sense of belonging to – of being an integral part of – *an ancient women's movement coming into this era through a hole in time*. It is as if time had been set, like an alarm clock, for the return of this women's awareness. But I really had no idea what I was really thinking. Not back then. In the decades to come, the picture would further reveal itself.

The scene of the flaming rainbow test these women had performed on me stayed within me.

The sky was perfectly clear, and the young man with the leaky boat was at the lake shore, as if he had been waiting. I approached him and requested that he ferry me back, fearless now of possible marooning mid-way.

We crossed the lake rapidly and with no problems – and with no water in the boat – a relieving positive development I could not explain to myself. It seemed that the boat had been healed, as if it were a living thing that had gotten well.

Once across, I paid the young man a few coins and found a small hotel where I could stay for the equivalent of fifty US cents a night, which was good as I was now living on some seventy-five cents a day. I had no sense as to how long this trip to Uxmal and everywhere else would actually take, and therefore, I watched every penny.

The next day, I began my inquiry into this Esquipulas directive I had received from the old bruja. Indeed, there was to be a great gathering there, in about three weeks. Although it was called the "Cristo Negro" or Black Christ Festival, it was more than the celebration of what was considered a miraculous event involving the sudden turning of a white alabaster Christ figurine to a dark-skinned one some hundred years ago, and also long before that, many other hundreds of years ago – again and again in time. Clergymen, salesmen, con artists, shaman, and medicine men and woman from tribes all over South and Central America would be there. I decided to go, feeling the deep magnetism of the mass migration. I planned to leave in a few days.

I could feel the tug. After all, my path was ordained. The trajectory was obvious.

Or was it? Well, yes it was. Although unfamiliar, the pull was so profound I could do nothing but respond.

14.
SEVEN rays to truth

My unusual time there was well spent.

While I waited to leave, I explored the mountain regions, making my way into a past that modern development had not yet compromised. I was absolutely enchanted by mountain towns such as Chichicastenango and Momocastenango, places back then still dancing with ritual and humming with the energy of indigenous magic. I was stepping right into another era, but more than that, into another realm where the ritual and the magic of the ancients ruled. At that time, this whole area had hardly been touched by the corruption of modernization. In the years to come, the tendrils of development would reach in, too far in. Realities we humans desperately need to preserve would be encroached upon, subsumed, driven in to hiding. Among these realities were the accesses to, portals to, other dimensions, spirit realms.

All this time since I had arrived in Guatemala, I had not eaten more than a few nuts and fruits. I was thus quite *wakan* when I was roaming around Momocastenango. I wandered, by mistake, into a funeral procession. Feeling attracted to the beautiful procession, which I thought at the time was just some sort of parade, I stayed with it. There I was, this tall, skinny American girl stepping into the atmosphere these beautiful people created with their intensely, even feverishly, reverent chanting. I was oblivious to how much I stood out among these shorter, more weathered, older in so many ways, remnants of an ancient and great people. I was alone there. I was a fish out of water. And yet, in my way, I was *wakan* along with them.

I walked and walked and walked, stepping through layers of sacred veils, slowly being permitted to see and to touch what was really going on there. I exhausted myself. Light-headed and tripping downhill along a winding, steep and tiny cobblestone street, I finally arrived at a large market. The first thing I saw was a walled-in area with a sign on it saying *"Prision de Mujeres."* I wondered what this might mean. Prison of women?

I was just about to sit and rest when, as I breathed in deeply to catch my breath, four men walked by carrying the thoroughly skinned and bloody carcass of a large water buffalo on their four sets of shoulders. The meat was obviously not fresh. The stench filled the air in all directions. Repeated waves of fierce nausea came over me. I would have been sick to my stomach but my stomach was empty. I was gagging fiercely nevertheless and my dry heaves were loud enough to draw a crowd around me.

"Bite this," a man's voice insisted in a sharp English with a Spanish accent, "bite this." He held out a wedge of orange. I nodded a yes, but was too sick and dizzy to reach for it. He put the orange to my mouth.

The sweetness distracted me from the smell. Then he handed me some mint, pressed my hand which held the mint to my nose, and insisted, "Let me help you get out of here." I nodded in agreement. What else could I do, I was feeling so sick? We walked out of the market and down the hill to the bus.

"I can't get on the bus right now, but thanks," I told him.

"Okay, would you like me to wait to help you get back to where ever you are going?"

"No thanks. I'll wait until I feel better and then catch a bus. Thank you very much anyway."

He looked at me, wanting to offer further assistance. Then he shrugged and left me his card in case I needed anything else.

I finally got on the bus.

When I finally got off the bus, I still had to walk the few miles back to the little hotel where I was staying. It was some walk. In a jungle sort of "hut-burbia," I wandered from block to block, through family parties and pastoral scenes. There were quite a few local people in the streets, heading back to their homes from shops or fields, visiting friends, looking for food in some cases. I merged with the loosely knit crowd as I walked along.

A fierce boom sounded.

When I heard the explosion, my first reaction was that it was relatively far away, was only some boiler going haywire, and was merely echoing nearby. Only after I turned the corner and came into a small bloody chaos did I realize that the sound had been a bomb and that it had gone off right there. From one block to the next, there had been a transition from peace to war, or maybe to a guerilla war, I did not know. Gunshots were being fired and people were running in all directions.

Another explosion sounded. Across the street, a telephone pole and sparking wire fell to the ground, causing the small mob to turn like a pack of frightened cattle and run – now all in the same direction – away from the sparks.

I was swallowed by the frenzied cluster of frightened people. I got caught in this surge of panicking humanity. The mob washed me to the end of a small side street. There I heard other people coming toward us from all directions. My instincts told me to get out of there, but it was not clear to me which way to go. Gunshots were approaching from about a block away. And then another explosion.

In rushed a stream of soldiers, their guns ready to fire – at us!

I was trapped in a swarm of confused, and by the aggressive looks of the soldiers' faces, officially expendable people.

Again I looked around for a safe exit.

A hand grabbed me and yanked me off the street, into a hiding space behind a shack. "You must get out of here right away," a raggedly dressed man with what sounded like a German accent warned in English. "Stay away from the crowd. Go down through that yard, and out the back of that house there, and then head into the main part of town."

We had a hasty and heated conversation:

"Who are you and why should I trust you?" I demanded hurriedly.

"Oh, you are an American chick. That's what I thought," he said in haste and disdain.

"What makes you think you know what you're doing?" I insisted.

"I'm one of the ones they're after."

"The European terrorist people?" I cringed visibly – I couldn't help it. Now I was disdained. "I've heard about you. What are you guys doing, killing people to make your point?" I turned to get out of there.

"Hey, young lady," he grabbed my arm, "Isn't there anything you would kill for?"

I didn't answer. I was scared.

"What about die for, young lady?"

I didn't know what to say. What would I die for?

"What about freedom? Would you die for your freedom?" There was an urgency in his voice.

"Well, yes, maybe … depending on what the freedom was." I heard some gunshots a few streets away.

He whispered quickly, "You Americans, you take freedom for granted, because you think you are free! Wouldn't you die for FREEDOM … THE FREEDOM TO BE FREE? FREE TO ACCESS SPECIAL DOORWAYS AND AVENUES, PORTALS TO OPPORTUNITY? This is your birthright, young lady." He let go of my arm.

Birthright? Portals? I wondered what to do. I wasn't certain he had any idea of what he was actually talking about, or of what my true birthrights were. Did I? "Well sure, I guess so. Of course I'd die to be free." I suddenly remembered being ready to risk my life to break out of Fire Star Tribe captivity, and cringed.

"Look, I'm sorry, you can't help being ignorant. I won't hold it against you. Maybe I'm the one who's supposed to tell you what's really going on on this planet."

Another one of these people who think they know what none of us really know, I said to myself. "What do you mean?" I asked quickly. I heard angry soldiers chasing frightened people, and all this approaching.

"Wake up. Look around. These are considered disposable people. So are we, you and I. We are rats in a cage on this planet, and it's going to get worse if people like you and I don't fight back."

Now several people near our hiding place were forcefully dragged off by soldiers.

"But killing isn't the way," I argued. "It's such a macho thing."

"Macho ... what's macho?"

"A male answer to problems ... violence ... killing ... rape."

Another gunshot sounded, this one far too close for comfort.

He stopped and faced me. "Look, young lady, until you women take over and show us a better way, we have to keep going with what we've got. Well?"

"Well what?"

Somewhat screamed. The terrorist went on as he grabbed me and started pulling me toward a doorway behind us. "Are you ready?"

"Ready for what?"

He yanked me through the doorway and through a dark and stinking room behind that doorway. I gagged at the stench. I sure did not want to know that this was.

He went on, "To take over – to lead the way. You know you girls complain about how we do it, but you haven't in a big way yet stepped in to help protect the very freedoms you want for yourselves."

When I didn't answer he pulled on me harder and said, "Well?"

We came to another doorway, this one leading into an alley stranger than all others I had seen. I looked at him, at a loss for words.

"Now go that way," he directed me.

"Why?"

"Up to you lady. Follow my advice and be safe, or run around here and get shot. Remember you're an American, an ugly American. But, even so, and even worse for you, you could be mistaken for one of we terrorists. Then it's death or a prison stay worse than death."

Seeing no other shelter, and wanting to get away from him, I followed his advice. Sure enough, and most fortunately, I found myself on an eerily quiet street and was able to get from there back to my little old hotel in relative peace. Panting, shaken, bewildered, but in relative peace. Guerilla wars in Central America could be like that in those days (and still now if we look) – fighting on one block and peace on the next. I was troubled by what the European terrorist had said, and I went over his words again and again that night.

The next day, I went to the post office to send some packages to the US. For some reason, perhaps standard protocol, I was asked for my identification. Once I showed the postal official my passport, he frowned and took it into the back office. I waited and waited and waited. When he did finally return, he did not have my passport. He said it would be investigated and returned to me at my hotel, and then asked which hotel that was.

I tried to reason with this man, in Spanish, of course, and then asked to speak to his boss. But whoever had my passport was apparently no longer there, having already taken my passport to some central office for further examination.

In the several days that followed, I continued to inquire about my passport and continued to be told that I had to wait at my hotel for just a few more days. I felt trapped, held, by an anonymous face, very much against my will. But, I decided to keep a low profile.

I wanted desperately to get moving, to follow my quest on to Esquipulas, and to not be confused with the terrorists. I was rather worried, but I made the best of the situation, and let myself transfix upon the myriad exotic sights and scenes of the area. I found myself distinctly drawn to the lake to see the sunset that night and the next night as well. Something very close to magic happened right then, at this time each viewing: when the sun set, the lake changed, it came to life – it grew almost visible wings and rested like a living thinking thing, poised in the volcano basin which housed it. I saw the lake alive, ready to leap, wishing to fly.

I met a man there, at sunset, a Guatemalan artist who was painting the scene. He described the event to me as "*un occaso de sol,*" an occasion of the sun, and it was at least that. In the moments immediately after I met him, the sunset sent out a cascade of Seven rays, rays of shifting colors, transforming from the brilliant standards of the rainbow to a mystical mix of an exhilarating orange, a brilliant yellow, a riveting chartreuse, a gentle turquoise, an iridescent blue more sky blue than sky, an ultra indigo, and a most magnificent luminous magenta. The rainbow danced and came to life, almost literally streaming its light across the receptive horizon and onto the living lake. And then, the entire place lit up in a fantastical silver-coated sheen, washing a cleansing stillness over everything it touched. Like a fragile almost impossibly high chord, this sheen held impossibly long, its overtone's quivers permeating the atmosphere. And then finally this sheen was collected, sucked back in, by the gravity of the departing sun. I looked around and the native people, the fishermen, and the women who washed laundry on the lake, were as transfixed as I was. For just a moment, we were all one, owing to the magic of panorama, at play in the realm of the Seven rays.

Times like this, you think you have brushed with Creator. Or *Maka* has. You've got to just love being here on this planet.

Times like this.

part four:

passage to the throne

Volume Two: Maka Shan Saga

15.
changing of the guard

The next afternoon . . .

... I wandered out through the devastation of the terrible *tremblor* -- earthquake -- that had hit just before my arrival in Guatemala. On my way, I realized that I had only been in this country a short time, yet it seemed to me to be an eternity. Dizzy, I sat down to rest and protect myself. I was raw – open – unshielded. Unwittingly in high *wakan*. My veil was down. I had hardly slept and I had not eaten. I had been so determined to find whatever keys – passages – teachings – I might find, that I had forgotten the normal aspects of living. I had surrendered myself so entirely to the quest that I was fully within it.

I stood up to walk on. Step by step, I became increasingly aware of how, with each passing day, I had shifted more and more deeply into this *wakan* state of receptivity to the spirit realm. So, state of mind is as important to the pilgrimage as is the pilgrimage itself, I murmured.

I instinctively chose to watch the third night's occasion of the setting sun from the ruins of the recent quake where hundreds of indigenous Guatemalans – descendants of the ancient Mayans – had been killed. I sat at the mouth of what appeared to have been a well and a fountain, surrounded by a mix of destruction and beauty, death and color. I could see how rapidly the jungle was growing in where ever the man made structures had collapsed. Dazed by the extensive rubble and the haunted atmosphere of the place, I hardly noticed myself begin to pantomime the ceremony I had learned from the old women on the mountain, and from the ancient version of myself, when I passed through the hole in time.

I was able to detach myself from myself only somewhat, but it was enough to observe, from both within me and without me, that I had slipped into an automatic series of gestures and whispered invocations, most of which were unintelligible to me. I did catch myself saying *"trsrt xulahhah ndndndnnahh"* – welcome to the portal – in that strangely familiar language I had come to know was buried in my subconscious, Wazine. However, I was in no way surprised by this, or surprised by knowing this chant. It all seemed eerily entirely natural. As I proceeded with this dual form of consciousness – this semi-alert semi-trance state – I found myself fully engaged in conducting this precious ceremony, and felt as if a powerful energy from somewhere beyond what I could see was coming through me. Something was running through every branch of my nervous system, reorganizing the very electrical charges and polar orientations of the molecules forming my cells. I suppose I was in an ecstatic state, yet I was so transfixed by the experience that I had no free second to be ecstatic, thrilled, impressed, or frightened. I just WAS what I was communicating. I WAS the message coming through me. I WAS the instrument of transmission.

I grew to feel I was being watched. Curious about this, I pulled myself a little more out of the semi-trance state and a bit more into day world consciousness. Now I noted that, sure enough, there were many eyes upon me. A number of native people had gathered around me. I was, at first, embarrassed. But then I realized they were not laughing at me. I studied their faces. Among them were the three women – *brujas* – I had met on the far side of Lago Atitlan. K'nah'koo'd-ah, the weaving one, nodded at me. For some reason, it made sense to me that she had appeared here. Surely, the Weaving One would weave and travel these realities across time and space.

And then, as the sun was laying its last rays across the land, I felt a distinctive cool rush I had known before in my life. This was the rush of beating wings. The cool rush of angel wings! Every time a portal – a passageway to the spirit realm – had opened, whether or not I had realized what was happening, I had experienced this rush.

Oh my! I blinked and peered into the air around me. There, right before me, was an old ghost of a woman, pretty much a ghost. Following her were people who had been at some ceremony I could see I had once led, way back in time: people dying, birthing, landing, coming and going from this dimension. I looked around and saw hundreds of spirits from all the different places I had thus far been during my pilgrimage, including the spirit realm I had entered with my old guide, the man named Kiowa. The spirit people were almost formed into physicality, but not quite materialized. They were surrounding me, and moving in closer. This sight was so rivetingly awesome that I was far too engaged to even feel my awe.

Near them, several living people were crying. Why? I looked at the closest person to me, an old, old woman who saw the question in my eyes and said, *"Mire, nosotros familias que meurten en el tremblor."* Look, our families who died in the earthquake. She pointed at the earthen rise a short distance away.

There were hundreds of spirits there, appearing to be the ghosts of dead men, women and children. These were the dead families! I heard a voice in my head – or was this Seven voices in unison I asked myself. They have come to this hole in time, seeking safe passage – deliverance!

A silence came over everyone gathered there, both disembodied spirit and spirit with flesh alike. We all, automatically, in the same instant, looked up at the sky and fell into a sort of silent group prayer as we gazed at a small vertical rainbow. This little rainbow was moving across the land like a beam. This beam was coming from a hole in the clouds which were gathered at the horizon – a hole looking something like a doorway. A portal. We all watched unblinkingly as this beam moved closer and closer to the ground, and as it made its way down to the end of the ruins where we were gathered.

This beam was composed of Seven rays, each one a waterfall of light, washing down from the heavens. The moving light fell upon us like rushing water. No one moved. I was spellbound – almost physically transported – right through that doorway in the sky by the mystic physics of this event. Feeling myself (or at least my attention -- it wasn't clear to me which) begin to lift off, I grew unsteady and sat down.

The old woman who had chanted over me on the far side of the lake now stood next to me.

I collected myself and realized, with great frustration and regret, that I had just then backed away from my chance to go home to the stars. I stood up, really ready now. I actually wanted to go there – to the heavens – to the realm beyond the veil. I looked at the doorway, began weeping with joy, and shouted feverishly and repeatedly: in this odd Wazine language I somehow knew, "*Moo-tah-hoh Tehrr-ha, vozhlahz wo meestirhey-yah*," Mother Earth, take me, send me home. And then I said in English, "Oh my God, I've found the keys to the portal!" And in Wazine, "*Trsrt xulahhah ndndndnnahh*," Welcome to the portal!

Completely beyond caring who was watching, I repeated these words over and over, jumping up and down, waving my arms as if to signal someone in the sky, expecting to be transported away at any moment.

The old woman who had chanted over me caught my Wazine words and seemed to understand. She put her hand on my wrist until she got my attention. I stopped my invocations abruptly and, finally minding that I had been seen acting this way, grew gravely silent. I stared at the doorway in the sky. That was my way home. I wanted to use that doorway.

She told me, "*Ahora, no*." Not now.

Why not now, I've come such a long way for this, I cried inside.

"*Tu tienes su Trabajo.*" You have your Work, the old woman answered as if she had heard and understood my thoughts.

My Work. The Work!! I thought of the directive of the Seven. How could she know of this? The Seven! "They're probably hanging around here somewhere," I muttered to myself.

Sure enough, as soon as I looked for them, I saw the Seven! They were silhouetted in that magnificent, awesome doorway from which the rainbow had descended. I could indeed believe my eyes, because I had become accustomed now to seeing such visions. Invigorated by their presence although frustrated by their holding me down here on this planet, I waved my arms intensely, resuming that deliverance ceremony I had once seen myself conducting. "Okay, you want deliverance," I shouted to the Seven in the doorway, "I'll do this deliverance thing, for God's sake! Fine, here goes deliverance."

I looked at the Seven in the sky. "What makes you think I know what I'm doing? I don't know what all this is! I don't know what's happening to me!"

Yet, I went to work, delivering. Immediately after I began this ritual, which was being driven and instructed by some instinctual directive buried deep within me, I heard thunder in a distant corner of the sky. I felt the ground shake just a little. It could have been the force of thunder that shook the ground, and the thunder itself could have been random, but what happened next undermined any remaining sense of "only coincidence" that I may have entertained.

182

A fierce, almost deafening, drumbeat sounded deep inside my head. A stampede of what I thought were running people raced through the drumbeat rhythm, through my head, and out into the day world. I blinked, startled. When my brief blink completed, there was the full half-animal, half-human, image of that chief I had once escaped from, Fire Star, flanked by his cadre of warriors, all hovering some distance before me. In that moment, I realized that I had not given them much thought since I had arrived in Guatemala. It had been a welcome respite. But now, alas, they had returned. Had they been watching all along? Had they been stalking me on my quest?

Even though they weren't here in the physical dimension, I could tell that they were here to stop this ceremony.

Why? I wondered. Why would they want to do that?

"The passage of the spirits is the Work of those who rule the realm of passage!" Fire Star shouted into my brain. "We rule and will not surrender to the Wazine."

You've got to be kidding me, I said to myself. "No one rules the realm of passage. This belongs to all of us!" I argued without speaking. I wondered if I knew what I was talking about. I was trying not to panic. The people and spirits around me were watching me with hopeful eyes. I couldn't let them down, could I? I could feel there were immense things at stake here in this otherworldly (or what some say was only imaginary) confrontation.

Fire Star must have read my hesitation and momentary questioning of the reality of all this. "Best you weaken by registering all this as imaginary, only imaginary. This is how the reality of what all this is about escapes most of you. You people don't see the truth about the spirit world, and so should not be allowed in. We will stop you now," he threatened.

"Over my dead body!" my inner voice shouted to these Fire Star men. I knew right then that if I closed my eyes to this reality in disbelief, Fire Star would win. I had to believe in this reality in order to participate in the shifting of power that had to take place. The shifting of power. The shifting of power. The shifting of power.

The Fire Star men began to close in on the scene. Stubbornly, or divinely inspired, I am uncertain as to which, I waved my arms and resumed the ceremony, moving myself in and out of the trance state required to remember its details. As foreign to me as it was, it was all quite natural. The dead families began to move in closer. Fire Star and his warriors moved to block the doorway to the heavens.

Now K'nah'koo'd-ah ran forward to my side, stomped her feet and shouted something I could not understand. She clapped her hands. A huge bolt of lightning struck right amidst the party of Fire Star and his men. They turned on her, poised to attack. I felt I should take action but was unclear as to what to do. What did I know about inter-dimensional struggles? What?

While I deliberated, every single woman within sight, whether in or out of her flesh – so-called dead or alive – moved forward to form a tight circle which included K'nah'koo'd-ah and me. Again, K'nah'koo'd-ah stomped her feet, shouted and clapped her hands. The women forming the tight circle mimicked K'nah'koo'd-ah in unison, stomping their feet, shouting, and clapping their hands all at once.

Hundreds of bolts of golden lightning came down around Fire Star and his men. They looked around, surprised. Fire Star faced me, not only surprised, but very ready to retaliate.

I marveled that I now knew exactly what to say from my psyche to his. "This is my domain," I told him. "You have no power here. This is the portal to the spirit realm that you no longer control. *YOU LOST YOUR POWER TO ME WHEN YOU RAPED ME.*" I was shocked by this realization as I spoke it to him.

He lunged toward me. I wanted to run, but did not. K'nah'koo'd-ah waved at the women to summon the lightning again. They did so. It hit the warriors hard. The warriors exploded into bits of light and evaporated. The half materialized Fire Star landed a few feet away from me. His hands extended toward my throat as if he planned to reach in from the ether and grab my physical dimension throat and strangle me as he once did in the flesh. As if to intercede, the women summoned the lightning yet again. Would their magic be enough to save me? I quickly glanced around their circle as they repeated their gestures. Standing in their line was a flickering image of Sveeka. She appeared and then faded, appeared and then faded. She completed the last gesture along with the other women and then was gone.

Just as I yelled, "Mommaaaaaa!" the lightning came again, striking Fire Star right atop his head. I thought he would explode as had the warriors. Instead, he transformed to a small ghost of a boy and lingered, bewildered.

My eyes grew wide in awe of Fire Star's transformation, in awe of Sveeka's appearance in the middle of all this, in awe of the logic of this vision, in awe that any of this had happened at all, in awe, in awe, in awe. I proceeded to conduct the deliverance ceremony, also in awe that I knew – somehow instinctively remembered – how to do so. I felt I was on some form of higher level automatic.

The families that died in the earthquake formed a procession and began to move through the doorway in the sky. I narrowed my eyes as if to better see the ethereally luminous distance into which they traveled. For a moment, I thought I could make out the unforgettable figure of Sveeka leading the way, serving as the guide, or handmaiden, of their ascension. The cool rush of angel wings rose and touched us all, leaving us glittering. It was so beautiful watching the families go. They left a short-lived but distinct trail of chalky light.

Of course, I said to myself. Of course? Yes, of course, these people had a right to their ascension. They had been trapped between worlds, needing assistance gaining access to the spirit realm. I was in no state of mind to wonder about this, I was so taken by the firmness of my conviction. I looked at the image of the bewildered boy, little Fire Star, as he faded away. Who would keep anyone out of heaven? I wondered quickly. He had apparently thought he would, could and should.

Heaven? After all, could I really still use this word? Why not? Just another name for the spirit world....

There was absolutely pristine stillness until all of the families had ascended into the clouds. Then the door closed. The sky changed. The local people began to walk away. Peace was in the air. It tasted like a divinely sweet elixir. Taste, what ever taste meant in this suspended state. But my tongue could definitely taste this.

Overwhelmed with joy, exhilaration, awe and relief, I sat down and cried … and cried. It had become so easy for me to cry.

The old woman, K'nah'koo'd-ah, waited there, alone, until I was finished with my tears. I looked up from my place on the Earth and smiled. She extended her hand and we touched fingers. "*Trsrt xulahhah ndndndnnahh,*" welcome to the portal, she said nodding.

"*Trsrt xulahhah ndndndnnahh,*" I replied, not wondering how she knew these words I had been hearing, even speaking since I was a baby.

"*Este es su paiz muchos eras antes.*" This is your kingdom in many eras past. She added in Spanish as she made a motion as if to include all I could see.

She handed me another God's eye. "*Va a los ceremonias en Esquipulas ahora. Su viaje para el Siete. Y para las sacrificadas.*" Go to the ceremonies in Esquipulas. Your trip for the Seven. And for those who were sacrificed.

And for those who were sacrificed? Who? Who? **Who was sacrificed?** What?

I couldn't quite understand the term *sacrificadas*. Still, I wasn't surprised at K'nah'koo'd-ah's directive. I had entered the delicate state of mind one falls into when so much, so real, so profoundly stunning, has happened so repeatedly, so connectedly. Now there was no question any more of its veracity. I kissed her hand. She chuckled.

I wandered off to my little old hotel room, walking in circles until I arrived. You do this sort of thing after a profound contact. Wander. Of course, wandering is not really the word. The next morning, there was a postal official at my old hotel looking for me and apologizing for detaining my passport. I had again been mistaken for one of the European terrorists. He suggested I leave the area right away since I wasn't a revolutionary. Of course, I agreed.

I wasn't a revolutionary? Hah, little did he know. And hah, little did I know. An inter-dimensional revolution was emerging, and I was beginning to see this. It would be years from this point that I would speak formally on this matter, to my colleagues and friends. How this would be received is a story for another volume.

I never mentioned to this official that I now actually suspected myself to be a freedom fighter – but one of a different ilk, one whose weapons were not guns and whose victories would not be achieved by killing adversaries. Rather, the work was to compel them to see what was at stake. I was, after all, an inter-dimensional guerilla, slipping in through holes in time, fighting for a higher freedom. I was fighting for the return of power to the First Mothers, for women's access to their birthright magic, for their returning to this time in history after having agreed to do so long, long ago. This was going to be the time of their Great Return, the Great Return of their knowledge and power, of the truth about how to navigate the Maka Shan, the great rebalancing.

I was now absolutely certain that the catapult had long been sprung and my trajectory more than ordained. I left for Esquipulas the next day.

Moo-tah-hoh Tehrr-ha, vozhlahz wo meestirhey-yah. Mother Earth, take me, send me home ....

Maka.

Maka Shan.

Volume Two: Maka Shan Saga

16.
in the god's eye

I arrived in Esquipulas ...

... after a long and crowded bus ride, mesmerized by my own nausea and praying that I would emerge from the bus in one piece. I was unceremoniously dumped into a mob – a swarm – a compacted herd of people from all over Central and South America. I joined them, merged with them. I remembered having been to some very large events, but I had never ever seen so many people so packed together in one place. My initial response was claustrophobia, which puzzled me because I was outdoors. What was this gathering in the name of the holy? Obviously the *Cristo Negro* – Black Christ – *Quince Enero* – January Fifteenth – Festival was in full swing. As I began to move into what I assumed was the town, I felt a bit better. I still hadn't eaten, save for bits of fresh fruit and vegetable juices, in weeks. So, I was indeed still *wakan* – still open to the spirit realm – raw more than ever now to the energies just past the veil of the material world.

But being *wakan* in an adulterated environment, a milieu screaming with spiritual conflict and con-men selling crosses, is frazzling. I wanted to scream out, a lonely intruder in an already invaded world, a lost soul itself looking for deliverance, possibly even an ugly American in a world being compromised – no destroyed – by modernization. What were all these plastic things and sweet drinks for sale? What was this – a pilgrimage to a mecca of materialist decadence? Everywhere was the rampant debasement of the divine.

"Okay," I said to myself loudly in English, "go buy yourself a drink and maybe eat something."

I wasn't hungry but this direction sounded sane to me. I bought some *ceviche* – a dish of raw marinated fish – and a bottle of bubbly water. I was thirsty and drank the water eagerly although it tasted metallic. I was not hungry but had a bite of the fish. Being my first bite of food in quite some time, the experience of its taste was nothing short of ecstatic for me. However, the second bite brought me to the brink of vomiting immediately. I left my food without reservation, picked up my pack and ran desperately into an alley way where I heaved up what little was in my stomach. Would I ever be able to eat again? Was I really here anymore, I wondered.

Sick and hot and dirty, I wandered on. I felt too naked here – an unnerving defenselessness set in. I was a foreigner in a foreign place – a stranger in a strange land. But this was about more than being a stranger in Esquipulas. It was about being a stranger in this material plane, something I would only begin to make sense of years later.

Okay, so where is God? Where are the spirits? Where is this thing all these people have come to touch and feel? My inner voice demanded information I could not provide. And where am I?

"*Donde este el Cristo Negro?*" I asked a man selling Coca Cola. Where is the Black Christ?

He pointed up the street to the highest hill, a magnificent hill upon which was built a beautiful old church. "*El primero Cristo Negro esta alla, pero hay muchas otras Cristititos Negros circe de aqui.*" The main Black Christ is there, but there are many other little Christs that are also black around here. He pointed to rows of street cars selling little figurines.

I determined to get my self all the way up there, to this "there" where, apparently, the first Black Christ was housed.

As I made my way uphill, I could see how the town circled this single hill on which was built a large Spanish mission-style Catholic church. It seemed that all processions were headed this way. But all who dared make this pilgrimage to the heart of Esquipulas faced many cunning distractions. Or perhaps, according to some traditionalists, these were actually tests along the way. Everywhere I looked, people were selling elixirs and potions, icons and magical objects – a bizarre bazaar. Every so once in a while, I saw what I felt I had come to be able to recognize as a real medicine man or woman. These persons were not shouting their beliefs or marketing their wares loudly from carts and podiums. Instead, they were strolling quietly along, taking in the situation, assessing the energy, and calling in their own gods at every stop along the way.

I proceeded uphill through the throngs, being flagged down, stopped, even grabbed by those who would deter me, people attempting to sell me Black Christs as well as elixirs and talismans for every possible curse and prayer imaginable. Was all this a competition for souls – a sort of race for unclaimed or unchained spiritual real estate – or a mere debasement of the divine? Or something else?

At the entrance to the cathedral grounds, I almost tripped over a man lying on the ground. Just as I tried to apologize, beginning in English, "Oops, I'm sorry," and realized that I needed to switch to Spanish to be understood, "I mean, *lo ciento, pardonne me*," I noticed that he had no arms or legs. I did a double take and tried not to gasp. Still queasy and achy, I was feeling far too vulnerable to let myself see this. I was going to look away immediately, but I tripped again on something and almost fell over right onto him. I caught my balance in a sort of hairline save of face. "God, I'm so sorry, *lo ciento mucho.*"

He caught my eyes and saw that I was practically crying at the sight of him. "*Este no es un acto de Dios, Senorita*," he announced in a guttural voice. This is no act of God, Miss, he had announced.

I knew he was referring to his physical condition. But why was he saying this to me, I asked myself. I wanted to look away from him, to break eye contact, but I couldn't. He looked like a pirate – an armless, legless pirate.

"*Mis parentes, quando yo estuve naciamiento, cortar mis piernas y brazos....para a prestar para mi familia.*" My parents, when I was born, cut off my arms and legs so that I might beg for my family.

What? Who would do this? Feeling I could do nothing to help, I pulled out an American ten-dollar bill. He thanked me and asked me if I would put it in his shirt pocket instead of in the can on the ground, as it was such a large amount of money that someone seeing it might pick it up. I did as he asked, patted him on the head, and said "*Mivoy a ver el Cristo Negro*." I am going to see the Black Christ.

"*Pero, yo soy el Cristo, el Cristo Negro*," he said laughingly. But I am the Christ, the Black Christ.

"*Si. Yo intiendo*." Yes. I understand, I told him, but I really didn't know what he was getting at. Did he mean he'd been crucified? Nailed to an invisible cross by his invisible arms and legs?

"*Adios, Señor*."

"*Adios, Señorita, y vaya con Dios si es possible en este mundo*." And go with God if it is possible in this world.

"*Yo espero que es possible, Señor*." I hope it is possible, Sir.

"*Entonces, sin suelo, no hay vuelo*." Well anyway, he said, without a floor there is no flight.

The ground matters.

"*Adios*," I said again and walked, shaking, into the churchyard, thinking about his last words: without a floor there is no flight.

I looked up at the cathedral. Maybe it was just that the entire structure was painted white. Maybe it was the time of day or the fact that this church was on the highest hill in the city. Whatever the explanation, the building seemed to emanate light. People were feeding into it from all directions. I joined the throngs and was washed in. I headed into what I believed was the light and there I found what I at first assumed was darkness.

Indigenous people, those who likely had the greatest right to be there, were sitting, lying and kneeling all over the floor of this poorly lit temple-like environment, which was covered with so many candles that it was difficult to walk. Many were mumbling prayers over rosaries they held in their hands. There was chanting in multiple languages coming from all directions. Several people were hitting themselves with branches and throwing rose water over their shoulders. The smell of sweat and rancid foods filled the place. What could be happening here? Where was this Black Christ I had come all this way to see?

I could see White Christs, several of them. There were women crying at the feet of these White Christ statues, weeping -- and then carefully using their long black braids to wipe their copious tears from these feet. I was instantly mystified watching. I had to force myself to walk on. I was in search of the Black Christ, I reminded myself. I had been drawn here to find the Black Christ because in this mystically occurring Black Christ would be a key – a key to something I was searching for – access to knowledge or to a realm still vague to me. … I almost asked myself how any of this could be tied up with my search for what I had come to feel was my birthright.

But birthright to what? To the sacred portal of access to the higher realms? Was I just crazy? I tried not to wonder because asking myself too many questions was going to rattle me far too much. Of course, not asking myself was also unnerving. I simply had to rely on instinct, or something more powerful than that … something calling me on a very deep level … a strange mandate….

I roamed around, confused, disappointed at first, tripping over bodies in the dark. I wanted to pray too – to pray to something, somewhere. After all, I belonged there, too. I had made my way there, too. I stood still and squinted around, searching for something, anything that would be a sign I was on the right path. Discouraged, I finally murmured, "God, please. I am so tired and I came all this way. Please please please show me something."

"Can I help you?" a soft male voice with a British accent asked from behind me.

I turned and found myself looking up into the most magnificent pair of the most intensely blazing blue eyes I had ever seen, even bluer than my guide Kiowa's or my father's. These eyes were those of a tall, alabaster-skinned, white-haired priest dressed in white from head to toe. For a moment, he seemed to be a tall thin white blue-eyed flame. He was virtually gleaming, and this was odd because it was so dark in there.

"Uh … well … yes sir, uh, Father. I came to see the Black Christ."

He smiled. "You are an American."

"Yes."

"California?"

"Yes, how did you know?"

"Just thought so. So you came all this way to see the *Cristo Negro*?"

"Yes."

"Well, he certainly inspires some particularly fine pilgrimages."

"I don't understand."

"Look around you. The Black *Cristo* you are looking for is everywhere."

"I really don't understand."

"Come, let's sit there a moment." He beckoned me to follow him to a pew, which I did.

"Well, young lady, what is Christ now is what is to be resurrected in each one of us, and in all of humanity."

I wanted for some reason to debate this and had the childish gall to try, "Well, I'm not so sure that imposing Christ on these native cultures is, or was ever, the right thing to do."

He blinked, a little surprised at my direct albeit relatively polite attack.

"The great *Cristo*, the Christ we speak of, walked these lands, these Americas, long before the Christ the Christian people worship was born."

"What? I don't understand," I said, trying to hide both my absolute incredulity and my total emotional exhaustion. Now I wanted to just curl up and go to sleep. No more searching, no more inquiry, no more questions. All this was too much now. I was verging on overload.

"What is your name, might I ask?"

"Lillith … sort of …."

"Interesting name." The priest smiled gently, trying to disarm me.

I grinned sheepishly. "Well, no."

"Weew, what parents you must have to give you such a name. Especially you. You must be grateful."

I immediately felt a wave of guilt, as if I had lied to this priest about my name. "Well, actually no. And I took another name." Right? Did I?

"Might I know this name?"

"Sure, but I don't use it. It's … uh … uh, Akashakana."

"Akashakana. Lilith of Akashakana? Oh my, you do bring the pilgrimage of the *Cristo Negro* an unusual treat."

"Sir, I mean father, I mean, I don't know what to call you, but none of this conversation is making any sense to me, and most of my life is making no sense to me anymore these days."

"Excuse me. Child, I am Father Posthumous."

Before I could stop myself, I blurted out a laugh. "You are indeed telling me a joke."

"No, actually, this is my name. Fancy that."

"I'm sorry, I should not laugh. Think of my name. It's even more preposterous."

"No, not exactly. You were named Lilith for a reason, perhaps a reason clear to your mother, and maybe even your father. Seeing you on a search for access to the realm, well this is so very much what Lilith would be doing now. Returning to take her rightful place in the realm."

"I really cannot follow you."

"Lilith, as the ancient Jewish tradition tells us, was cast from the kingdom of Eden once she declared herself entitled to the knowledge and power available to at least Adam if not to God. She has been waiting, for eons and eons, to return and claim her power. This is her time, you know. And there are many of us ready. And there are many women on the journey you find yourself on, Lilith. This is a lifelong journey you know. Many lives long."

I stared at the women cleaning the feet of Christ, wondering if I would break into a million pieces at any moment. Why was what this priest was saying so tough for me to hear? Why here? Why now? Why tough?

"Yes, some of the women here in this part of the world reenact the Biblical washing of Jesus' feet, seeking inerrancy, as close a translation of the Bible as is possible. But, the truth is that many others are reenacting – and even mourning -- what they view as the sublimating of a polytheistic Goddess worship by not Christ but by --"

He paused a moment to see if I was really following him. I really wasn't, but I apparently was following enough for him to finish his sentence: " – by all that was done with Christ's life and story, by all religions on Earth."

For some reason I could not explain to myself, I balked, "What you are saying is not very Christian or Catholic. I'm surprised that you are telling me this. How do you know I will listen? How do you know my religion – whatever it is – will let me listen?" I wasn't even sure whether I would really listen. At the same time, I was absolutely fascinated, virtually enthralled by the concept this priest was presenting. At this point, I had no idea whether I had a religion at all.

He looked extremely patient now. "I know. No matter what your belief system, this is strange to hear. ... Christianity is a complicated thing. Far more complex than those of us who thought we understood it ever imagined. Take for example those women over there weeping onto the feet of the White Christ."

I looked at them again.

"This is not simply a replaying of what some people believe to be the Mary Magdelene story, in which she washed the feet of Jesus with her tears and then cleaned his feet with her hair. This is a ceremony of far greater import, at least to those who know."

I watched the women with greater attention now. I could see that their tears, while flowing freely, were part of a purposeful ritual. There was a logic to this. I was feeling it, but not knowing it. A vague sense of recognition filtered into me. On some deep, ancient level, I knew what all this was really about. I knew this priest was another form of medicine man who happened to be wearing the robe of this label.

"Poor Mary Magdelena," this priest said. "The Book of Luke says Jesus expelled Seven demons from her. Could these demons have been something else?" Now Father Posthumous peered mysteriously at me, as if I actually did know the answer.

"Seven?" was all I said.

"Seven."

How had I arrived here, right now, for this meeting with this way past typical priest? And why, oh why, I wondered, was I hearing this bizarre information right then? Things were confusing enough. I had been propelled on a strange enough journey, on an almost desperate search for something almost impossible to define. And now this new deconstruction of my old and even my new reality was taking place. After all, although I had rejected or thought I had rejected all Judeo-Christian influence upon my life, even abandoned the much maligned name, Lilith, what this priest was telling me was really shaking me up.

"What I am trying to say is that one man's demon may be another woman's spirit."

I shook my head no, and was not certain why. No? Yes? No? Yes?

"You see, while Christ may have been imposed upon these people by the earlier European missionaries, and while the plan was to impose Christ upon these people while leaving as much of the native culture in tact as possible, something else happened. An entire civilization invaded and thought it was rightfully, in what it thought was its God's name, conquering another, taking over another's sacred lands. What folly."

"I don't understand." What was he talking about? Why was he telling me all this? Was he rewriting history? Or proving history's lie? What?

"Nowadays, at least some of us have come to understand. We were finding out more about the Cristo than we would have ever known had we not thought we were bringing Christ to these truly Native Americans."

"This isn't making a lot of sense to me," I told him, puzzled.

He nodded. He seemed to emit waves of peace and serenity, as well as a remarkable luminosity that I could not explain to myself.

"I was wondering, how long have you been here?" I asked.

"Most of my adulthood. I came for a tour of duty when I was a young priest, and then never left. This is my home now. These are my people. Or better stated, I am theirs. Do not be fooled by what I wear."

"You mean you're not really a priest?"

"What I mean is that this many years here has taught me the greater story, a truth stretching well beyond the boundaries of any one religion or myth."

I was silent. Tears were in my eyes, trying not to be cried. I could feel his ultimate truth reaching me.

"Are you lost, child?"

"Lost?" I whimpered.

"Lost."

Because he had asked me, I realized how very lost I was. "Yes, I guess so," I answered unsteadily, wondering why so many tears were now pouring out of me.

"And you came here in search of the way?"

"The way?" I tried to stop crying so I could make sense out of this conversation. What was he getting at? Was he going to try to preach to me, was he some kind of evangelist?

"The way. We all look for the way, a way, into the spiritual realm," he said in such a kind voice that I was immediately wanting to hear more of its tone, no matter what its words.

"Spiritual realm? Like heaven? Like beyond the physical?"

"Yes, the way to seeing more of this world than what the eye normally sees. In this, in finding this, being lost is part of the journey, a key passage."

"Well yes, and more. I came here because I want to go home."

"Are you lost then?"

"No, but the place I want to go is not on this planet."

The priest did not seem surprised. He touched the left side of my chest above my heart. "Well, child, home is, after all, where the heart is."

I felt his words, through and through. HOME IS WHERE THE HEART IS. "But I keep feeling like I don't come from here, from this planet. It's making it hard to put a life together."

"And yet you are leading your life."

"Well, barely."

"Perhaps this IS your life … the great pilgrimage … the quest for the divine … the journey home through your heart back to—"

"Back to the stars," I interrupted.

He looked at me with those glowing eyes. As he did, I felt a powerful undeniable wave of compassion wash over me. This wave of beautiful energy was coming from him – or through him actually, and seemed to be a cloud made of the energy of pure love.

"What's that feeling?" I asked. "You sent me a feeling, didn't you?"

"The feeling comes through me and through you. It comes from home. Take it with you wherever you go. Share it. Magnify it. Spread it here on Earth. When you need it, one day, when you do leave this planet, you can follow it like a thread, a map, all the way home."

Floods of tears started pouring from my eyes again now, washing down my face in torrents, like overflowing streams in a heavy storm. An intense wave of sound came over us, a wave of chanting by the people conducting ceremonies on the floor amongst their oceans of candles. But this was more than a wave of sound – it was a wave of feeling, a wave of awareness, a wave of being at the door to the spirit realm. I saw the priest close his eyes, reel a little in the wave, and chant along with them for a moment. Then he returned his attention to me.

"Why do you stay here?" I asked him.

"I will stay here until I die. If I can help even a little to correct the great misunderstanding of the European invasion, I will do so. Europeans were so wrong about what they were doing in the Americas."

I looked at him, trying to fathom what he was saying.

He continued. "This is my way home now. This is my family. These are my teachers. These are my Gods. I live with these spirits."

I stared at him, trying to consume what he was telling me as if I had been hungry for it, starving for this version of the sacred, for so, so long.

He reached into his pocket and pulled out a tiny, precisely woven God's eye, which was attached to an old rosary. "I would like to give this to you."

A priest with a God's eye? I reached into my pocket and pulled out mine. "I would like to give this to you."

He accepted and examined the God's eye I offered him, eyed it a moment, and then looked at me with surprise. "I see you know K'nah'koo'd-ah, the old *bruja* in the hut up the mountain on the far side of the big volcano crater lake north west of here. She makes a very distinctive God's eye like no other."

"K'nah'koo'd-ah? You know that woman? She gave me that God's eye. I was there at her home, where she weaves. She told me to come here."

"For many years we have known each other. This is quite a coincidence."

"You may call it that. I can't."

"Of course it isn't." He took my hands in his and held them gently. I watched his face as he closed his eyes and sat in silence for several minutes. He opened his eyes abruptly. "Oh my," he whispered, "I see ... yes, I see ... you must go to Uxmal."

I almost fell off the pew. "Uxmal?" Now someone else was directing me to this Uxmal place. "Why?" I wondered and then reminded myself, that female government agent had also, although more secretly, told me to go to Uxmal. Somehow, this Uxmal journey was an order from fate.

"This is for you to discover. It is between you and the ancient spirits who guide you, dear one." He paused to study my face. "But what is it? Why do you look so very surprised?"

"Because, K'nah'koo'd-ah and a few other people – people I've met for the first time while I've been on my way wherever it is I've been going – these other people have also told me to go there, to Uxmal. And I just don't get it. What's at Uxmal? What's going on? Why is this happening to me? The first person who told me to go there was a very short gnome-like man I met on a freight train in the US, who somehow saved my life when I became very sick and couldn't get any medical help."

The priest raised his eyebrows and then seemed to get it, what ever this it was. "Uxmal means built three times, you know, or you may not know. When you go there now or in the coming times, please do look beyond what tourism will do to Uxmal. And when you get there, if you can, go be there at the nunnery, a large building named Nunnery by Europeans who did not understand that this place was built as a school for healers, shamans, priests, medicine men, and yes women. But the real teachings for the women were secret, even within that culture. … You will also want to go to the House of the Magician, also named this by Europeans who did not understand what power the ancient medicine held. And also go to the House of Old Women, another European name of course. Look beyond what people there may say, and find this place for what it truly is, find its truth yourself and --"

The priest was interrupted by a sudden synchronous loud wave of high toned wailing by the women washing the Christs' feet, more like long wails of screaming. The priest sat up very straight and listened.

When, a few moments later, the screaming wails diminished, the priest looked at me, intently. "Never mind, Lilith of Akashakana, never mind these details. Just get yourself to Uxmal, the rest will become more clear."

"I do not understand what --"

I was interrupted by an event of lighting, a magnificent one.

The sun must have positioned itself just right at that very moment, because now a light ray broke in through a very high, tiny opening in the wall. It spilled down, brushed the sides of our faces, hit the ground right next to us, and splashed into a rainbow. As it did, I thought I felt a wind slipping in through an open window. I looked around and surmised that there were no open windows. Must've been the cool rush of angel wings, I told myself. Again, I gasped as I got the message.

The priest was watching my reaction. "Ah yes, the *arco ires de las Siete rayes*."

I interrupted, "The rainbow of the Seven rays."

"You know this sign then?"

"Well, I don't know exactly what I know, but I do, I guess I do."

"Of ancient and eternal significance to these people, to the indigenous people of all the Americas, in fact, to all the world. And now it is the harbinger of the message emerging to take us through the end of this grand era."

I heard a voice – no, it was Seven voices in unison. I recognized these right away as *the* voice of the Seven – speaking inside my head. "This is a message for the turn of time," they said.

"What does this mean?" I asked the Seven aloud.

The priest must have thought I was speaking to him, or wanted to pretend he thought this, because he chuckled and acted as if he was answering the question I had asked of the Seven: "*Sed quando submoventa erit ignorancia—*"

"What did you say?" I asked him.

"What did I say? I was saying, 'When the time comes for the removal of ignorance ...' "

"Then what?"

"When the time comes for the removal of ignorance, the case shall be made more clear."

"I'm not sure why you said this."

"Oh, well, really it was the mystic French prophet Nostradamus who said this in Latin back in 1555: 'When the time comes for the removal of ignorance, the case shall become more clear.' "

"But what does this mean?"

He smiled at me. "You will know what this sentence, and much of the rest of all that you have seen, means when the time is right for knowing."

We sat in still silence for many minutes, as long as the rainbow lasted.

"Was that rainbow a sign or something?"

"The covenant, the arc or light, the arch of light, the wand connecting us to the spirit realm."

"Oh," I tried to assimilate all this.

"And also a sign."

"Sign?"

"That one of the First Mothers has returned to *Maka* for the reunion."

My eyes widened. *"First Mothers? Maka?"*

The priest put a finger to his lips, "Shhh! I should say no more. But, welcome back, Lilith of Akashakana." He leveled his blazing blue eyes at mine and held my gaze. Somehow, I was instantly transfixed. I could not have looked away even if I'd wanted to. As I stared into his eyes, the face around his eyes changed from old to young to man to woman to some form of androgynous being from the stars. I felt information being moved from way beyond us, way past Earth, through his head, through his eyes, into mine. It was like getting a book I couldn't read, but knowing one day I would be able to decipher the language. This went on for what seemed to be a long and a short time. I thought that everything around us had stopped and that all the people in the cathedral must have been watching.

And then, deafening thunder broke just over the cathedral. I understood the transmission from the priest to me to be complete. I stood, bowed at the priest, and mouthed, "Goodbye." I knew that was what I was supposed to do right then.

He also stood. *"Dona nobis pacem.* Grant us peace," he said and nodded.

"Peace?"

"Peace rather than the Great War. Or better yet, a peaceful form of the Great War, a Great Rebalancing. This is what we must work toward. This is part of The Work."

For some reason now, I was not even a little surprised by this comment. Not here, not now, not surprising. "Yes, *dona nobis pacem,*" I repeated resolutely. "And yes, peace rather than the Great War."

"Yes, this is the real revolution. Peace on Earth. Finally peace. And peace to and from Earth, in all dimensions."

I nodded gravely and turned to leave the cathedral. I looked back a few steps later and he was still nodding at me, his tall white presence standing out in the cathedral, singularly alone in the crowded space. I nodded back at him again.

I wanted to see him one more time, so I quickly turned back one more time, but he had vanished. I had no idea how he could have left so quickly, but he had.

I left that day. Another profound meeting with another profound guide who had appeared out of another profound nowhere. Another who had touched my life in a profound way. Another one I would probably never meet again. Not here, not in the same form, not in this lifetime anyway. Or?

After so much profundity, I was beginning to hunger for the mundane. But I was seized by a directive far larger than my little wish for a little relief.

Finally, I accepted the directive: onward to Uxmal.

17.
the great return

Sheer instinct drove my migration.

Indeed, I was now most driven to proceed from Esquipulas to Uxmal. The Earth was calling me there; I could feel the pull in my feet – a mysterious but profoundly magnetic tug. At this stage of the journey, I didn't question this pull toward a place I'd never been. I just left Esquipulas and made my way to Uxmal. Back then, tourism had not yet compromised the resonating truth about these areas, or their magnetism.

On the plane from Guatemala City to Merida, Mexico, where I planned to catch a bus to Uxmal, I gazed spellbound at the majestic mountains below. We were flying through an awesome wilderness of clouds and light. A while into the flight, the plane began bouncing, as if hitting large rocks as it traveled through the air. The bouncing was almost enough to make me seasick. I had to concentrate on warding off more nausea.

But the bounces turned to small but disturbing falls and then the small falls to unusually long and unusually frightening drops through holes in the air. Fear began to get the best of me. My palms gripped the rickety armrests. Staring out the window, I could hear the walls and wings of the plane rattling the same way the old ramshackle bus to Atitlan had. Abruptly, we dropped what seemed to be thousands of feet toward the Earth. My stomach went into sharp spasms, and I began a series of dry heaves. As there was nothing to speak of in my digestive tract, there was nothing to come up out of it. Abruptly, we shot upward what seemed to be the same thousands of feet, then the plane shuddered and creaked and seemed to almost roll on to its side.

"Just become the wings," a voice next to me said in a Dutch British accent. "Just become the wings and fly the plane."

I turned to the source of the voice, however I couldn't focus on his face. I felt as ashen gray and green as I must have looked. The plane dropped another what seemed thousand feet. I tried not to scream the way people do on roller-coasters. Another dry heave wrenched through me. I bent over, my head in my lap. The plane was groaning as if it was about to crack in half. I heard the man next to me shouting to me, "You'll be fine. Just become the wings and fly us home!"

We tossed and turned. People were moaning, gagging, and vomiting, and beeping stewardesses who weren't coming. An unsecured overhead luggage bin fell open, spilling its contents down onto the aisle: a radio losing its batteries, a broken doll, its head rolling down the aisle, wrinkled papers, a smashed hat.

"Mother Earth take me, send me home," I muttered to myself. No, not right now. Not by crashing to the ground.

"Fill yourself with light and you won't feel sick. Start with your stomach," the man next to me tried to get through to me.

I decided to listen to his advice. Why not? What was there to lose?

I closed my eyes and imagined a ball of light in my stomach. At first, it was a vague flicker. It took a few moments to fill out the image but, once I did, I found myself hanging on to it for dear life as we rocked and rolled and dropped and toppled back up and then down again, each time falling farther it seemed.

At some point in the middle of all this, during a rugged drop through the air, the light expanded like an out of control balloon and filled me throughout.

"That's right, just expand until you fill the entire plane," I heard that man say.

I let the light expand beyond me, encompassing everything near me first and then working its way down the aisle and outward into the body of the plane and then even into the wings. "Woah," I yelled out.

"Got it?"

I nodded a yes with my eyes still closed.

"Good, now fly us out of this, please."

His request sounded silly but urgent. At a loss for other options, I let my imagination expand into this illusion and soon I was in the cockpit at the controls.

"But I don't know how to fly," I shouted. Or do I, I wondered in desperation, remembering that I had told my father that he had taught me to fly.

"What?" the man asked trying to hear me over the rattling and creaking of the old plane.

"I DO NOT KNOW HOW TO FLY!" I opened my eyes and yelled.

As the plane toppled what seemed to be a mile or more, the nose of the plane dipped down and, for a moment, I thought we were heading into a nosedive. Now even the man next to me looked frightened. He grabbed my arm. I looked a little more closely at him. He must have been about sixty years old. I felt his grip on my arm and realized his palms were sweating. He was scared, too.

Oh, geez," I said to myself, this is not good. This guy's more scared than I am.

We bounced hard to the right and then upward and then down and then up. My stomach, empty but sick, was in my mouth. I needed to go back to the light. Obviously the man had done all he could to help me. He was now dealing with his own fear. Or was he?

I shut my eyes and found that the light imagery I had generated was still with me, exactly as it had been when I left it. I forced myself to concentrate on this to ward off this horrible fear. Okay, back to the cockpit. I took my mind's eye there. "But I don't know how to fly," I shuddered. Wait, this is just my imagination, isn't it? In my imagination, I can do anything. We fell again – another mega-drop – and then bounced violently higher in the cloudy wilderness.

"Take me home. Please. Take me home." I was so scared I couldn't think of a way to calm myself.

And then, voices seeming to come from the clouds outside the plane were sounding in my ears: "Not right now. You have Work to do."

"Who are you?"

"Seven."

"The Seven?" Here?

"Yes."

"Well then, please, take me home. Now. Please. I'm ready. Just lift me out of all this."

"Not right now. You have The Work to do. The Work. The Work. The Work."

I started to argue when a distinct rush of what at first seemed to be air and then light came over me. It seemed to come into me, as well, and to course through my veins, a sort of benign form of electrocution.

Quivering, I opened my eyes a second and glanced out the window right into – right into – what a sight! I was immediately transfixed and all the fear dropped away. A beautiful circular rainbow! A beautiful circular Seven-ray rainbow. "*Las siete rayes*," I whispered. "*Las siete rayes. Las siete Rayes.*" Somehow, I just knew this circle was a portal.

Now we hit another violent passage through this knotty wilderness of air and light and clouds. I shut my eyes and felt myself slip right through the center of the rainbow. On the other side, I WAS the plane and I was its wings. I was its captain, but not from the cockpit, from the intelligence of the body it created through space and time. I was a plane made of light and there, in that chalky reality, I knew that I was a pilot – a navigator – of that dimension. I knew I could stabilize the energy and take all of us on the plane along with the plane itself – as a single, large body of light – down gently and whole. I didn't let myself know anything but this. Why wonder? Just believe.

It occurred to me that this was arrogant of me. But if this perception would bring me peace and perhaps even safety, why not? And maybe, somehow, the picture I was seeing would help other people. Maybe they would feel it somehow.

It was a magnificent, magnificent experience. The most magnificent of all magnificent experiences, I was thinking then. I felt like a huge great winged bird made of a white light, flying through a long cylindrical rainbow tunnel. I thought I felt the big rush of giant angel wings – the wing wind of a great white bird. White wing.

Oh my! Was this the dove? Kiowa, old friend, great teacher, where are you? Sveeka, what about you?

"Sayeth my name if thou wouldst travel upon me," I shouted. "Name?" I asked myself. Name? Oh! Rushing water. Rushing water. Rushing water.

Like rushing water, nothing moves. Like rushing water, nothing moves. Like rushing water, nothing moves, moves, moves. Now I could hear Sveeka's voice chanting this reminder in my ears. What did she mean?

"OH! OF COURSE!" I shouted to myself. "OF COURSE! JUST <u>BE</u> THERE AND WE WILL GET THERE. BE LANDED … CALL THE SAFE LANDING IN AND WE WILL HAVE LANDED SAFELY!"

I think I lost some time, which can happen when you fold it. I remember nothing of the next minutes, nor how many of them there were after this point.

Everything stood still.

Some time later, we landed calmly. I opened my eyes and felt well. Very well. And full of vibrating light. I wanted to thank the man next to me. I tuned to him and saw that he was still white and quite pale. I started to speak, but he said something first.

"Thank you, captain. You delivered us safely."

At first I laughed, thinking he had made a joke. Then I saw he meant what he said. "Delivered?" I asked myself. Delivered? Delivered? Oh, deliverance? "Mother Earth, take me, send me home," I murmured.

"Pardon me?"

"Or someone bigger than we are delivered us." I went on chanting under my breath: "Mother Earth—"

"What are you saying?"

"Oh nothing, just a little prayer I know."

As we headed off the plane, I resisted the powerful temptation to kiss the ground. Instead, I just let my feet touch it, feeling the solidity, the blessed physicality, of the Mother Earth through my shoe soles. Ah, *Maka*. I noted that she was a little electric. This vibration startled me. I knew it from past experience. This had to be sacred ground! Right here at the airport, under the asphalt runway. Mother Earth, I thought. *Maka*.

"I feel like kissing the ground," the man who had been sitting next to me was at my side saying.

"Me, too."

"Where are you headed?" he wanted to know.

"Uxmal."

"Well, how about that, I am going right by there. Can I give you a lift or do you have a ride?"

"Well, no thank you. I'm taking the bus."

"Perhaps then I can take you to the bus … in gratitude for the great landing you made for us."

I laughed a little.

He seemed serious. "Oh yes, that was you who flew us in. Sure wasn't me," he insisted.

"More like the spirits who protected us," I answered.

"Through you," he smiled. "You were the gateway, channel, portal for that light."

Portal? "Me?" Portal? I walked on a bit, with this odd man next to me. Who was this guy anyway, I quizzed myself, half hoping the Seven would hear and answer.

"So, it's Uxmal, is it?"

"That's where I'm going, but I can get myself there, really. Thanks though."

"May I ask why Uxmal?"

I stopped and looked at him. I shrugged. "Sort of a personal pilgrimage, I guess." I realized I had no logical explanation for him or for anyone including myself. "I'm just running on instinct." And voices in my head, I added silently – on a divine directive.

"Hmmm, Uxmal. Funny thing is, I'm going that way anyway, as I said, to visit my daughter and granddaughter. I offer the ride as a friend."

I studied his face. I could see he was sincere. He was a kind man, older than my father, with very pale skin, white hair, and blue, blue eyes. I decided to accept his offer. "Well, sure then, thank you."

The ride was relatively uneventful, except for the fact that I discovered that he, Joseph, was Dutch, yet had lived in Mexico for fifteen years and many more in South America before that. He was a fountain of information and knew the ancient ruins we visited along the way surprisingly well.

We stopped for a drink at a small jungle *tienda* – shop – under a palm-leaf *palapa*. A small boy ran up to us, asking for *un poco dinero* – a little money. He was holding a portable radio to his ear, turned up full blast. It was a toy Volkswagen bug with a large antennae protruding out of its hood. A cola commercial began blaring from its window. The man I was with nodded a yes, and said, "*es para ti, para ti es esto dinero.*" He then asked me to pull his wallet from his jacket which lay on the chair next to me. As I did this, the wallet fell to the floor. As I scrambled to pick it up, it opened and some of its contents showed. I saw some kind of badge but I didn't ask what it was. Strange. A man with a badge was transporting me. Again.

I couldn't stand the sound of the commercial on the child's radio, so I went outside. I headed around to the back of the *palapa* to better see the jungle. There I found a man examining some bones and a skull in a carton. Alarmed at my sudden presence, he glanced up at me, ready to run. For a moment, I thought he was the gnome-man I had met on the freight train, but he didn't seem to recognize me. I took a step toward him and he sprung up, grabbed the carton, and ran into the jungle, dropping a few bones along the way.

I went over and looked down at the bones. I pushed a round one over with my foot and was revolted at the site. It was a human skull! And next to it were the bones of a hand. For some reason, I just stood and stared at these remnants of someone's body. I had no idea why, but for some reason, I heard myself saying, "These could have been mine."

I heard Joseph calling for me to return to the car, so I composed myself and decided to say nothing about what I had seen and how revolted I had been. We continued to Uxmal. Now I was glad I had company.

At Uxmal, we got out of the car and decided to hike in on a narrow path. Tourism and development had hardly touched the ancient Uxmal back then, in the 1970s. I knew little about the place and Joseph didn't offer much in the way of information. Although the jungle vegetation looked typical of the vegetation in that region, this place was somehow different and definitely eerie. We were alone there, no other inhabitants or visitors were to be seen.

I walked along behind Joseph, who had been there before. I became increasingly entangled in the fronds of the jungle. It's not that the plants and vines and branches were tripping me and wrapping around me, but some kind of invisible extension of these life forms was weaving its way to me, engulfing me and catching me up in its elaborate matrix of energy. I fell further and further behind Joseph, who looked back once or twice and inquired, "Are you all right?"

"Oh, yes. I'm just taking in the nature in solitude, I'm fine."

"Sure you are all right?" he asked again from up ahead.

"Sure. Thanks. I'll catch up with you in a while."

"See you up ahead then," he shouted as he disappeared.

I later grew close to Joseph and his family. Eventually, one of his friends told me Joseph was a US government agent, maybe CIA. Eventually, Joseph himself told me that he had found me when my passport was being held back in Guatemala.

But today, this day at Uxmal, I knew nothing about this man other than that he was a very kind guide. His wisdom would reveal itself to me long after he passed on.

18.
sacred opening

Finally then, Uxmal.

Tourism had not yet paved walkways, so we were on a narrow and rough trail to the site. At that time, I didn't think much of Joseph's disappearance way up the trail. I was, after all, walking very slowly. His death some twenty five years later (which is yet another story) would vastly unsettle me, but not his disappearance on this day. I liked being alone there. I had always liked solitude. But here there was more to what was going on with me.

I was beginning to feel the ground vibrate rhythmically with a steadily increasing intensity. The sensation that I was being shocked was reminiscent of the electrical shock sort of sensation I had become aware of when I had touched the ground at the airport only hours earlier, and also when I had lived in the sacred territory of the Fire Star Tribe land. I was beginning to hear Earth speak. I was beginning to connect with – even to merge with – the ground. *Maka*. Again, as I had several times already on this pilgrimage, I felt as if I were walking through rings of time, back, back – back into what, I did not know.

Joseph hadn't told me that this was once where selected Mayan women, young ones, who had prepared throughout their lives for this sacred event, were ritually sacrificed. No one mentioned to me that the deep holes in the ground were old *cenotes*, many of them now empty of water – some of them where these sacrificed women – *sacrificadas* -- had been killed and given to the spirits.

Given to the spirits ... the spirits ... the spirits.

I thought I heard a whisper somewhere among the vegetation. And then I thought I hadn't.

The spirits ... the spirits ... the spirits.

Being *wakan*, journeying onward in my lifelong *hanblechaya*, some sort of walkabout, I was indeed light-headed. I was indeed hypersensitive to energies not readily distinguishable to the normal human perceptions grounded in the material realm. The veil was down, way way down. I was tiptoeing now, stalking the Gods themselves – unaware that I myself was being stalked....

I thought I heard a vague but eerie scream, up close but far away. Startled out of my naïve reverie, I whirled around. But I was alone on a neglected dirt path through a tangled jungle full of untold secrets.

Time was riddled with receding voices, women of eras past, ghost calls of long-dead priestesses. The announcement was unmistakable ... ancient races were dying.

I felt an uncanny pressure on my chest. A powerful yet invisible hand was pressing into me. For just a moment, I couldn't breathe. I opened my shirt at the neck. The thick semi-tropical humidity was getting to me. The jungle wanted to swallow me, I could tell. I could feel the heavy air pushing my skin as if to collapse it – to dissolve it. Would I give way to the unseen pressure and just melt? I had to wonder.

I was road weary. I had been on a long and desperate search for something I couldn't quite define. I still didn't know exactly what it was, but I could still feel it calling me. So many directives along the way had egged me on to its discovery. I had no choice. I had to make the connection … I had to find the key. I had been put on the path, initiated into the quest, and there were no exit signs. There was no opting out, no turning back.

Now, gasping for beads of drier oxygen in the hot wet air, I almost missed the brilliantly marked snake slipping between my feet. The obscure sound of his sleek skin sliding across the moist and fertile ground hit my ears. I froze. Make no noise, I told myself. I looked down and saw him. His head turned up toward mine. Are you poisonous? Are you going to kill me, I wondered, too alert to be frightened. He looked me in the eye coldly, as if to answer. Clearly, the next move was up to him.

I silently made my peace with the situation. Maybe I would be dead in a moment. I wasn't surprised at my acceptance. After all, I had died so many times on this journey. All right then, Mother Earth, you can take me, send me home. Fully engaged in my surrender to the choice of nature, I forgot to be silent and whispered aloud the words I knew so well, "*Mah-kah-hoh Tehrr* -- "

Obviously startled, the snake shot his head right up the inside of my leg past my knee. I halted my chanting in mid-phrase. He must have heard the vibration of my words, I scolded myself. He stopped. "Now what," I asked myself. This was not the normal kind of confrontation. What do you do with a slimy wild animal when you don't want to be attacked by him? It's a problem, especially when you're in his territory. I racked my brain for an answer, but only instinct could save me. Giving way to the cutting pressure of the moment, I exhaled abruptly and the rest of my whispered chant burst involuntarily from my lips, "...*ha, vozhlahz wo meestirhey-yah.*"

What happened next will never leave me. The snake jerked his head back from my leg. I thought he was about to strike. Then, he lifted his head a foot higher into the air, as if to hear me better. I, being at a loss, and being caught in the madness of the moment, started whispering again – this time very slowly and carefully – to the snake. "*Maa-Kah-hoh Tehrr-ha, vozhlahz wo mee skan-hey-yah.*" The snake froze. And then it came to me that my only hope was to chant him into either submission or boredom, which ever came first. If it didn't work, I would have at least tried. And if he killed me, I would at least not be dead for the first time.

Aside from the obvious life-threatening danger I was in, we – this creature of the jungle and I – were a funny sight. Now I was the snake charmer. I repeated my phrase again and again, whispering in English and in the phrase's native tongue: "Mother Earth, take me, send me home. *Maa-Kah-hoh Tehrr-ha, vozhlahz wo mee skan-hey-yah. Mother Earth, take me, send me home. Maa-Kah-hoh Tehrr-ha,*

228

vozhlahz wo mee skan-hey-yah." As I did, I found myself lulled into a detached state. It seemed that I had hypnotized myself and perhaps the snake, too.

Time went on this way, until, after I had chanted at him for what seemed hours, although it was only part of one hour, the snake seemed to have had his fill of staring at me and suddenly slipped back down to the ground and whisked away.

Just like that. He was gone. Numb to the reality of what had just happened, I hiked on. I had come all this way, was still standing, and wasn't going to turn back now because of a snake or anything else.

As I walked on, I went back to thinking about my long search. I had started out at the age of just barely eighteen, when, on the path of naïve idealism, I stumbled into a political-spiritual cult – a radical Native American commune located in Northern California. There I began my rocky entry into adulthood, shortly after my mother died. There, I had suffered the collapse of my identity, my reality, my dignity. Against the muddled back drop of ritualistic reverence for what I was told was the sacred, and rebellion against what I thought was the "establishment," I had been raped by the leader and held captive by the community. I had balked, and then had been treated as fallen, fallen from the position of chosen one. I was trapped, I was miserable, I was sick and in danger, and I almost died. Yet, while all this was happening, I made contact with my self and my ancestral line in a way that I might have never otherwise done. And, I was trained in indigenous ways, shown worlds unseen, initiated into the spirit realm, taken deep into some of the most protected esoteric teachings of ancient America. I had, against my will, traded my flesh for the key to precious but heavily guarded teachings.

And it was there that I had been recognized. In my unsuspecting adolescence, I was seen for who I had been in another place and another era. My cover had been broken. I had been caught coming back into this time to keep my commitment to a cause so vast and so etheric that I could barely fit an emerging memory – a fragmentary admission of it all – into my immature consciousness.

I stumbled over a rock as I walked on through the loud jungle, reviewing all this.

And now I had been drawn to – directed to – this ancient place they called Uxmal. A mysterious hand in time had pulled me there. I truly had no idea that this was where the ancient Mayans had sacrificed their priestesses, and that this was an honor that these young women had prepared for all their lives. I truly had no idea that it was these women who, in concert with a cadre of other ancient priestesses from other ancient cultures and realms, had put out a call through time, beckoning me there. And I wasn't the only one being called to remember the reason for returning to the now.

I walked farther on, still reviewing my journey. Searching for something vague had led me to that point in time. And now what? Would this have all been for naught? And would the answer to why I had come there please make itself known to me?

I decided to try invoking the answer, much the way I had learned to sayeth the name of the river or whatever I wanted to have come to me: *"Answer come ... answer come ... answer come ... answer ... answer ... answer...."*

A wave of something intangible washed over me, halting my quiet invocation. Amazing, I told myself, I have learned the magic! Just as I somehow recognized that this sensation was actually time opening, I heard the vague eerie scream again. I wanted to be frightened but now I found I had a bizarre affinity for the sound. It felt hauntingly familiar to my ears. Had I invoked it? Is this invocation thing safe here in these unfamiliar surroundings?

I shook my head, laughed uncomfortably, and walked on, telling myself I hadn't heard a scream – I had only been hearing things. Things.

I couldn't stay away from this invocation thing. I wanted to try it again. Let's see, should I call the answer again? No, not that – it's too profound. Maybe I'll play a joke on myself and call myself. Yes, that's it! I'll invoke myself. I will sayeth my own name.

I started out saying, with humor in my voice, "Lillith, Lillith, Lillith ... ah ... ah Akashakana... oh right, Akashakana, Lilith Akashakana," and triggered a precise memory of the moment I – or the Seven and I – had once named my self in Fire Star's sweat lodge, evading Fire Star's naming of me: "I am Akashakana ... Akashakana ... fire dove ... Angel of Fire ... Akashakana ... Akashakana ... Akashakana ... Akashakana!"

I heard a voice in my head, sounding like Sveeka say, "And remember Lilith, you are *Lilith*. You are Lilith for us. Lilith Akashakana." I tried to ignore this message from my mother as I had much of my youth. Jubilation came over me, and I began shouting my name, Akashakana, at the jungle around me. I was calling myself to me, and I realized this within a gleeful sort of self-affirmation. I shouted to the trees, and the ground and the sky. Like a child discovering a new toy, I was having a really great time with this. *Sayeth my name ... sayeth my name ... sayeth my name!*

I tried to ignore my birth name, Lilith, but for some reason a troubling and demanding awareness of it crept up in me. It was just then that I thought I felt a cold hand touch my shoulder. I whirled around, and there was no one behind me.

I stood still, more still than still, filled with a certain and highly precise kind of knowing that I was perched, right then and there, on the very edge of my life.

"Of course, no one is behind me. There's no one here and that guy Joseph is way on ahead. I have to stop getting scared when I'm opening a portal," I advised myself, knowing so very little and knowing so much of everything about what I was up to.

I walked on, my heart wide open, through the rings of time, touching the Earth with my soul. I heard myself begin to chant in time with my footsteps: "Mother Earth, take me, send me home. Mother Earth, take me, send me home. Mother Earth, take me, send me home: *Maka Shan Maka Skan Maka*. I call myself to me. Akashakana!"

Again I felt a hand, this time pressing into me with a little more force. Again, I turned. Again, no one. I walked on, now feeling as if the Earth might electrocute me, her energy had become so wild. I had to say my name: "Akashakana."

My heart! I felt pressure on my heart, as if it had been grabbed! This made no sense to me, so I forced myself to ignore this as well.

I looked around again. The jungle really did seem to be growing faces – faces protecting ancient secrets. A wave of something intangible rushed over me. Just as I somehow came to know that this rushing sensation was time opening, I heard the eerie scream again. Now I found I indeed had a bizarre affinity for the sound. It felt more than familiar to my longing ears.

I shook my head, laughed uncomfortably, and walked on, telling myself I was hearing things. But then I thought I felt a hand again touch my shoulder. Again, I whirled around, and again there was no one behind me.

"Okay fine, I'm Lilith, Akashakana."

And then I felt yet another push – a real hard one this time. I almost lost my balance. As I whipped around and saw no one, I felt the sensation of a hand pressing down on top of my head. I brushed whatever it was that was touching me away, but there was nothing on top of my head.

"Lilith," I mumbled trying to distract myself now.

I started to turn and walk on when I felt far greater pressure on my heart.

My heart. A fist on my heart. Grabbing my heart! Grabbing? Pulling? Taking my heart out?

Pressing my hand over my heart, I turned and decided to walk backward for a few moments to watch what was going on behind me.

"Lilith," I whispered into the thick air, no more stubbornly than foolishly.

There was nothing and I felt silly. I breathed a sigh of relief and began to laugh at myself out loud as I started to turn back and face ahead of me on the path. I guess I'd better stop playing with this magic I was telling myself when …

Just as I let down my guard, it hit me – the biggest push into my shoulder – right through me – and I fell … a long long long eternal way.

I screamed that scream I had been hearing.

19.
falling through time

Into the next few moments...

...were stuffed lifetimes of impressions and eons of knowledge. I know this all happened very quickly, but time practically stopped along the way down. Downward, hitting my back and shoulder and head several times on the way, each blow seemed harder and hit in quicker succession than the one previous. Each jolt filled my head with color and pictures – pictures of some kind of ceremony, some kind of very intense last moments of my life.

My entire life seemed to rush before my eyes in that instant, however, it was not my life but the life of a young Mayan priestess in ancient times. She knew she was about to die in a ritual process and was in close contact with the spirit realm that had already opened for her before she was killed. Killed? I am not being killed, my consciousness screamed at itself. This is not me. No. No. No.

Everything stilled until time finally did stop entirely, with the immense gears of the universe coming to a grinding but gentle halt. I thought an incredible old woman was catching me in her reaching arms. The last blow to my head as I toppled into the hole was so terrifically hard, I passed out. The world went black.

Then there came a blinding flicker of brilliant light in which I saw the Seven with their arms extended what seemed to be upward toward me. Just then, time stopped – and Sveeka caught me in her arms.

* * * * * * *

I came to in this dry *cenote*, dead again. I expected to open my eyes – wake up dead – in the next world, and see the spirits, ancient spirits, all around me. Instead, I felt the gush of warm blood down my forehead into my eye, and down from the area under my right eye all over my cheek. I knew which life I was in and that I was alive. Alive in this lifetime I had been living and was still living.

But there was a moment of internal chaos, a moment of inter-dimensional shock and fierce confusion. I had been that Mayan priestess being sacrificed by that Mayan medicine man right there. I had willingly given my life back then *in order to return to this time where I was now*. Of this, I was thoroughly certain. This was the dawning of the time of the Great Return. This was!

We were all coming back.

We had to come back, to turn time. Had to for *Maka* and for all her people. For the human species and all living things on Earth.

I looked up out of the hole, right into Sveeka's immaterial face. "You're just a ghost," I said, "you can't help me out of here."

She pointed at my heart, where I had once dreamed I stored the crystal drop, the drop of pure truth she had once given me as I lay in despair on Fire Star's bed. I felt a blossoming in my heart, a warm overflow of light growing in there.

As if it had been a catalyst, the light of this truth illuminated a passageway. I found I could see through time as I lay bleeding at the bottom of that hole, that old once water filled hole where Mayan priestesses were once sacrificed, their hearts once cut out right before their bodies once thrown down, down, down into time. I could see Mayan priestesses and priestesses of other ancient tribes – Western, Eastern, Egyptian, and more – Lilith and Isis and famous Goddesses from all over – now gathered around the hole I was in, close to Sveeka.

Of course, they were telling me – communicating to me right through this hole in time – that for us to give our lives back then was the way to carry the power of ancient women directly to this time where you are now. This is how we are coming back now, back for the Great Return.

* * * * * * *

When finally I actually came to, I realized something immense, something that I would not have been able to accept prior to now: The young woman I had heard screaming in the jungle – this was me. That had been *my* voice calling at *me* through time. I had been that Mayan priestess being sacrificed by that Mayan priest right there. I had willingly given my life back then in order to return to this time where I was now.

I was thoroughly certain of this as I lay there bleeding through the ragged and filthy cuts in my head and face and body. My certainty filled my veins with an unimaginable strength in the face of an unimaginable degree of physical pain.

I was having trouble breathing. I felt again that pressure on my chest. When I closed my eyes, trying to breath, I felt a hand grabbing at my heart, tugging on it as if to pull it out of me. With my eyes wide open, I struggled desperately with the unseen. I wanted to keep my heart. I wanted to live, there, now. Here, this lifetime. I was indeed here to do The Work.

Realizations washed through me like sheets of roaring rain: Pictures came into focus in my mind like photos developing. These Mayan women and other females sacrificed around the world in ancient practices had secretly and carefully planned to go underground, to hide their true identities, to move into another dimension, to die or be killed if needed, to protect, preserve, and eventually reinstate, the power – the wisdom, the keys -- that their ancient sisters had lost.

I lay there in awesome pain. What? I asked myself as hot blood ran into my burning eyes. What? What? What?

I answered myself in words that were not mine: These ancient sisters were the First Mothers, the originators of all ancestral lines of true medicine women, the founders of all lineages of the truly high priestesses. These were the pre-patriarchal women leaders. And these were the women who had foreseen the suppression of their own power, of their magic, of their dominance – and, for reasons of all kinds, of the submerging of their kingdoms into the hands of men and the ways of men and the minds of men.

A logic that was not mine made its way into my thoughts as my eyes flooded with blood. These women had formed a secret sacred sisterhood. They had created a vessel for protectively camouflaging – and then passing on – women's potency from one time into another. They had constructed a means of reassuming the medicine and magic that was their birthright – when the time came. And they had carried their profound scheme down through the ages – into this time. And now here I was, along with the others who had sacrificed themselves on the altar of time, dead again, alive again, come to close the circle. Here for the Great Return.

It would be some years before I would even begin to step up to the commitment I had made so many eons ago, even start to see the plan. And Seven more years would pass before I would take on the real Work in an distinct way. And Seven more before I would truly break free of the binds that kept me from my full Work. And Seven more while my commitment to the Work was tested and forged. And Seven more and Seven more and Seven more and Seven more and Seven more and Seven more and Seven more and Seven more and more and more ….

In the meantime, it would be least several decades, if not more, before the "modern" world would come to grips with even some of its genocide of ancient peoples such as the Mayans, especially Mayan women and children. And it would be longer still before we would come to recognize the profound significance of these virtually invisible massacres. A quarter of a century later, people would mourn these lives against the backdrop of the extinctions of ever more of Earth's endangered indigenous peoples and species. Massacre and sacrifice would take on new meaning just as the human species was struggling to avoid doing both to itself. Terrorism and the fight against terrorism would evolve to an unusual level, as if Gods themselves were wreaking, or at least threatening, havoc on Mother Earth, on Maka.

And then these ancient women returning to the now would make themselves known. They would step forward, finding each other like clockwork, their cadre ready to march for the preservation of life, for the reinstatement of their life-protecting power, unfolding just in time, into the dying now.

I finally had the answer. For now, my search had ended there at the bottom of that dried-out sacrificial pool. I knew that I was not going to die that day. I had Work to do.

I lay aching and bleeding and waiting. Help arrived. My life was saved. Again.

They found me unconscious. I came out of the hole a new, albeit very concussed, bruised and cut up, young woman, and a very, very old woman indeed. The trajectory had been set, the path ordained, and The Work agreed to long, long ago. The time had come for the removal of my ignorance. Like rushing water, every fiber of my spirit was moved.

Ah yes, the Work ….

I reflected on my life as they carried me out of the jungle. Yes indeed, time had passed since that terrible night of apparent initiation into that tribal commune I once believed was access to sacred teachings, that night in that old house where at least this part of my journey began. I had been young and stupid back then, and I had landed in an awful situation.

Yet, when a medicine man rapes a woman, his power is transferred to her. And when man rapes Mother Earth, his power is returned to her. Yet, rape is not the highest mechanism for this return of power to its rightful hands. No.

That was a most unlikely place to begin a most likely unveiling ….

Like rushing water, every fiber of my spirit was moved. *Maka Shan.*

Maka Maka Maka Shan -- Skhan – Shan.

Maka Shan.

We shall not cease from exploration
And the end of all our exploring
Will be to arrive where we started
And know the place for the first time.

T.S. Eliot
Four Quartets:
"Little Gidding"

epilogue:
veils riding down

It's funny how a simple push can land you in a pool of profound knowing. Of course, sometimes you sit in the pool of knowing a long time before you recognize you are there. After all, knowing itself is not always conscious. Wisdom can come to us without our even realizing this is happening.

This story is continuing, beyond the point of my fall into the sacrificial hole in Uxmal, throughout the sacred and frequently bumbling pilgrimage I call my life, into the past, the now, and the future. I have on some level truly embraced the Work of the Seven ancient priestesses who have escorted me through this life down here on Mother Earth, Maka. This embrace has necessitated an oftentimes perilous balancing act between my material plane identity – career, reputation, family, friends, writing, teaching, et cetera – and my higher identity (whether or not I wanted to deal with it). Speaking openly about such matters is bound to raise eyebrows, especially in professional circles. People just don't believe things like this.

But I do. I have walked along the edge just far enough to know there is a whole and very real universe out there, a universe of many splendors and dimensions. And I know this universe to be quite

243

magnetic, compelling, alluring beyond the point of material plane logic. This has, naturally, made the normal progression of my otherwise normal and challenging enough life rather more trying. Others like me also know about this experience.

I have sought a seamless integration, of both the ordinary and the extraordinary aspects of reality, into my daily life. At the outset, this integration appeared impossible. Now, decades later, I know the effort to be one of the most fulfilling in life – yet one of the most potentially conflicted.

Okay, so there actually is an ancient sect of medicine women, priestesses of many teachings, who have been on this planet and elsewhere at various times before. Now, they are returning to Earth to re-establish the true power of the feminine. This is far greater than a woman-man issue. This is about a far greater true feminine. This is the much needed return of the highest of the feminine truths and keys for sustaining and protecting life, and even for protecting THE LIFE FORCE, for its survival in all dimensions.

True power of the true feminine is more than one more nomination to a corporate post or one more admission of a woman to chambers hitherto reserved only for men. (Of course, these are in themselves great modern advancements and increasingly prevalent now.) While I fully support these openings, I contend that these are openings to a world that has evolved within masculine constructs of reality, and of power, opportunity, rights, wisdom, and so on. The true power of the feminine has another texture to it altogether. It has a force far greater than imagined by so-called modern minds. It has a magic to it, a way of working with material things and situations in a non-material fashion. True power of the true feminine is not going to be resurrected simply by opening doors to the men's world, a world dominated by material plane matters.

So the priestesses are returning through time into the now, to also take their rightful places in the greater hierarchy. Yeah, right, and Tinkerbell was brought back to life by being willed into resurrection. We've come a long way, baby, but how far is that exactly? Each of us has to answer this question in our own way. I have had to answer this for myself, based on indications I have been receiving from all around, a constant barrage of hints or, better stated, signs.

So, I say this: There is something going on, something happening here. There are essences, or life forms, or intelligences, calling out to us, and even coming in to us. They reach us from outside ourselves, and they reach us from within ourselves. They do reach us.

The intelligences, or spirits, or priestesses as I like to call them, are coming back now, reaching into our times, having planned to do this long ago. They are making their appearance in our hearts and minds, in our worlds, now, for good reason. Look around, because they are some of us. In fact, now we are here in growing numbers, to do the Work. I'm here for this. Maybe you are too. Maybe you already know this. Or maybe you will be discovering this about yourself soon. Perhaps you have been drawn to this Maka Shan Saga because you are part of this story or a witness to this story.

And it's no party. It probably would have been easier had I chosen a particular religion – an existing one with some kind of social status – and labeled what I defined as inter-dimensional reality as my "belief system" as per that particular religion. As you will read in one of the sequels to this story, when cross-examined about what all this meant, a handy label of a pre-packaged and approved religion would have perhaps allowed me some relief under the auspice of my first amendment rights as per the US Constitution. These were rights I thought I could rely upon in this dimension (as future volumes of this Maka Shan Saga will explain).

Resurfacing ancient truths, pulling them into a resistant world, was never going to be easy, but was going to be far more than most necessary. And so it is. Stay tuned....

We are the Wazine Seven, of the Maka Freeborn Triton Line.

We have been nomadic spirits since our home base was destroyed. We move through time, galaxies and zerhatz, weaving the thread of true freedom.

We have been called revolutionaries, and we have been called witches. We have been called Lilith and Isis and Goddesses of all names. We have been called queens, priestesses, shamanesses, medicine women, and we have been called prisoners. We have been heralded, worshiped, exiled, bought and sold, sacrificed, burned at the stake. We have died on the streets, under bridges, in graves, in ceremonies.

We have given our lives while our hearts stood, still beating, in the hands of the men who killed us.

We are indeed soldiers, an army. Yet, the weapons with which we fight are made of purified light and fueled with the radiance of the divine that this light brings.

This is the turn of time. We are here to bring it in. We have returned from exile. Only the return of power on Earth to the original and most cosmic feminine can save the planet and all systems upon it now.

We are a wave of change returning to the now for exactly this to happen.

You can ride this wave with us, turn the tide with us, heal the rising of the Great War with us. Light is our tool, and it can be yours, your key, your access to realms long hidden.

Step forth, citizens of the new time, into the next leg of Earth's journey and the next stand of humanity's journey.

The future of humanity and human civilization, and of Earth herself, beckons. Our beloved Maka is calling us to the Great Rebalancing, to the Maka Shan, by the Great Return.

Maka Shan.

AFTERWORD
by
Dr. Angela Browne-Miller

This is the story of a young woman, Lilith Akashakana, whose life has somehow been pulled into a mysterious journey. This is the journey of everyone on the quest for truth about what is really going on now, in our lives, in our minds, in our souls, in the cosmos, and here on Earth. Where psychology and the sciences just do not explain it all, are there sources of knowledge elsewhere? Are there ancient secrets that explain us to ourselves, and explain our times to us -- even explain the possibility of power shifts and Earth changes to come, and the means of surviving these?

Who knows the truth about all this? Are we supposed to want to know these things now? Are we being called by something powerful, deep and invisible, being directed to know these things in our times? Or is all this just imagined, some form of fantasy or hype or scare tactic perhaps?

Yet, if there are secret ancient teachings that can save us, shouldn't we know the truth about these? And who has a right to access this truth? Here, in this novel, The Great Return, our heroine, Lilith Akashakana, is determined to access this information she believes is her, our, birthright. She travels to homes of ancient tribes such as the Mayans who know what she has been told is the true medicine and the true truth.

She has broken out of the normal path of life she has been expected to follow, and now is in search of meaning and truth, as well as of ancient survival knowledge teachings. Many events have taken place in her young life, including the recent death of her mother, and being raped by someone who said he had access to the survival teachings she was so intent upon learning. But now some sort of transfer of power has taken and is taking place, and Lilith is being called to know this.

Our heroine senses she is participating in, even perhaps one of the subjects of, this transfer of power. However, the deeper meanings of this transfer are both cosmic and personal. And so, as we read through this story of Lilith Akashakana's journey, we read through a metaphorical pilgrimage to higher self. Perhaps it is in this pilgrimage that not only identity but healing and even power can be attained by Lilith the individual, by Lilith the female of the species, by Lilith and all of us living on this Earth at this time, and by Earth herself. Perhaps.

Of course, we cannot overlook the comments about the return of a true feminine power to save the Earth and life on this Earth. Can it really be true that there is a cosmic feminine, a level of this essence well beyond what we know the feminine to be in our everyday lives? Here, in The Great Return, we learn that ancient priestesses are returning to our times to bring this higher feminine power in to save us, the ecosystem, the planet, and perhaps far more. Some sort of great rebalancing is being ushered in now. This is what Lilth Akashaka discovers. She is here for The Great Return.

Whether we read this story as an adventure, or a spiritual quest, or something still more profound, we are called to follow the path of search for self. After all, it is this search that can unveil great secrets. Of course, there are times when self-knowledge is not necessary or is even too much to process. The struggle of self to define itself and its world view is age old and ongoing. This is such a noble struggle. In the end, when Lilith Akashakana falls to the bottom of an ancient sacrificial well, she sees not only who she truly is, but who many of us truly are.

WHAT FOLLOWS THE GREAT RETURN?
LOOK FOR
VOLUME THREE of the
MAKA SHAN SAGA:

HEART WARS

AND WHAT CAME BEFORE VOLUME TWO OF THE
MAKA SHAN SAGA?
VOLUME ONE of the
MAKA SHAN SAGA:

MAKA SHAN

Written by Anatarra Whitewing
Afterword by Dr. Angela Browne-Miller
(cover on following page)

This is the tale of a young woman, Lilith Akashakana, who turns eighteen back in 1970. At eighteen, right after her mother dies, she joins a Native American commune, a pan-tribal tribe, seeking her true roots as she carries Native American blood herself -- a fact which her parents had seemed to her to be ashamed of. Now she feels called to find herself. She also feels called to learn the Tribe's Earth Change survival knowledge she has heard about.

However, she quickly stumbles into confusion and trouble, including rape, captivity, and near loss of life. She also discovers that the US Government is following her, and studying the efforts of some to regain access to sacred lands, portals. She is overwhelmed. Yet, she also finds some of the greatest spiritual teachers one could want to know on one's life journey. And one of these guides seems to be her dead mother, now reaching to her from other realms.

Once escaping the commune, leaving the dear friends and teachers she met there, she is directed by guides she finds along the way to embark on a journey to visit other tribal areas in the Americas, to understand the teachings she was given during the very trying time in the commune. She is called to ancient Mayan ritual grounds. She there finds, much to her surprise, that she actually belongs to an ancient tribe of medicine women who are speaking to her through time.

Published by Metaterra® Publications

MAKA SHAN

VOLUME ONE: MAKA SHAN SAGA

ANATARRA WHITEWING

Afterword by
Dr. Angela Browne-Miller

Readers, you will also want to look for the
BLOODWIN SAGA Collection
written by Alias Skye
VOLUME ONE of the
BLOODWIN SAGA COLLECTION:

PROJECT HEARTFIRE

Available as Kindle Ebook and Amazon Paperback.
(see cover on next page)

Fiction: Edgy sci fi, sex, obsession, and romance novel. Psychological thriller. Beautiful, brilliant, professional woman is invited to become partner in a futuristic business worth hundreds of millions. Then, her entire reality is shattered. She behaves unexplainably promiscuously, engaging in intense extramarital sex with two scientists, falling into an intense obsession with one of them, while the other is desperately in love with her, and while both men are working toward global domination via their cutting edge cloning business. Our heroine eventually discovers she has become hooked on a high tech drug which was developed to encourage clones to engage in sexual activity with humans and vice versa. Can she break her addiction? Can she fix her life? Does she know too many secrets about clones now? Are there clones walking among us now, all over the world, today? Read the novel and see.

**And also look for the
BLOODWIN SAGA Collection
Volume Two:**

BLOODWIN MANIFEST

Available as Kindle Ebook and Amazon Paperback.

Intriguing, exciting, and disturbing, Bloodwin Manifest is Volume Two of the Bloodwin Saga collection. This is an incredible psychological, sci fi, sex, and romance novel. Here, we find walking among us, almost perfect beings, seemingly perfect beings anyway, who are copies of others, clones. Already there are plans to use these clones to achieve control of the planet – of us. What is happening and what are we doing about it?

Read this novel on its own, or as a follow on to Volume One, Project Heartfire. Either way, you will be walked into a world you have never seen, or have not realized you are already seeing. Many readers will want to follow the characters we meet in Volume One, Project Heartfire: Risa, Gavon and Dan – or better stated perhaps—the several Risas, Gavons and even Dans, some of which may not know the others exist.

Books by the Author of the Afterword to this Book

ANGELA BROWNE-MILLER
http://www.AngelaBrowne-Miller.com
Also uses pen name:
DR. ANGELA DEANGELIS
(See these and other books by this author listed on Amazon.)

Endings are Beginnings:
Navigating Your Hard Times Into Higher States
Written by Angela DeAngelis.

Embracing Eternity:
The Life Force Does Not Die
Written by Angela DeAngelis.

Transition and Survival Technologies:
Interdimensional Consciousness as Healing, Survival and Beyond
Written by Angela DeAngelis.

Healing Earth in All Her Dimensions:
Personal, Species and Planetary Healing
Written by Angela DeAngelis.

Rewiring Your Self to Break Addictions and Habits:
Overcoming Problem Patterns
Written by Angela Browne-Miller.

To Have and To Hurt:
Seeing, Changing or Escaping Patterns of Abuse in Relationships
Written by Angela Browne-Miller.
Foreword by Arun Ghandi.

Will You Still Need Me:
Finding Friends, Love and Meaning as We Age
Written by Angela Browne-Miller.
Foreword by Evacheska DeAngelis.

Raising Thinking Children and Teens:
Guiding Mental and Moral Development

Written by Angela Browne-Miller.
Foreword by Evacheska DeAngelis.

International Collection on Addictions
Dr. Angela Browne-Miller, Editor.

Violence and Abuse in Society:
Understanding a Global Crisis
Dr. Angela Browne-Miller, Editor.

metaterra®
publications

The Publisher
Metaterra® Publications

Project Heartfire©, written by Alias Skye, is published by Metaterra® Publications for general distribution to readers all over the world. Metaterra® Publications is an independent publisher. For other Metaterra® publications, see the website:

http://www.Metaterra.com

**See Novels by Title Section
of the Metaterra.com website
and see also Amazon.com**

www.ingramcontent.com/pod-product-compliance
Lightning Source LLC
Chambersburg PA
CBHW051632260626
47170CB00004B/1151